CHANCE ENCOUNTERS

LISE GOLD

Copyright © 2024 by Lise Gold Books

All rights reserved.

No part of this book may be reproduced in any form or by any electronic or mechanical means, including information storage and retrieval systems, without written permission from the author, except for the use of brief quotations in a book review.

We sometimes encounter people, even perfect strangers, who begin to interest us at first sight, somehow suddenly, all at once, before a word has been spoken.

— FYODOR DOSTOEVSKY

1

ALLY

"Are you a member of our Frequent Flyers Club?" The ground stewardess labelled Ally's suitcase and typed something into her system.

"Yes. Sorry, I forgot." Ally searched through her wallet. Like her life, the bulging mass of leather overstuffed with receipts, crumpled bills, and forgotten cards was a chaotic mess, and it took her a while to find her membership card.

"Thank you. Just give me a moment." The woman frowned as she stared at her screen; Ally suspected her account had expired as she hadn't flown with the airline in years.

"Is everything okay?"

"Absolutely." The woman looked up with a smile. "Would you like an upgrade? Free of charge."

"Seriously?" Ally's dark brows shot up. She hadn't flown business since she'd resigned from her job three years ago, and she'd braced herself for a long, uncomfortable flight that would likely leave her exhausted by the time she arrived in Amsterdam. "Of course, I would love that."

"Excellent." The ground stewardess printed her

boarding card. "Here you go. Have a great flight, Miss Brenner. The lounge is a five-minute walk from your gate. Enjoy."

∼

Ally had missed the Emerald lounge at Vancouver International Airport, with its polished marble floors, the soft glow of recessed lighting, plush armchairs, and leather sofas that looked out over the runway. The familiar notes of oak and vanilla made her feel a little nostalgic as she secured a table by the window and removed her trench coat. She used to come here with her colleagues every other Monday, and although she didn't miss her old job, she did miss the perks of having a big travel budget. Running a small project management company with her friend now, Ally didn't splash out on expensive flights. Perhaps that would change if her upcoming pitch was a success.

As she ordered a glass of chilled Chablis and helped herself to a few salmon blinis and a small bowl of olives, she noted not much had changed. She even recognized one of the bartenders, despite him having grown a beard since the last time she had been there.

Heading back to her seat, a woman across the bar caught Ally's eye. She ordered a martini and took a careful sip before scanning the lounge. She had short, blonde hair and big, blue eyes emphasized by eyeliner. She wore a sharp-cut black suit, and a leather laptop sleeve was wedged under her arm. Their eyes met, and the woman smiled. There was something familiar about her, but Ally couldn't recall ever meeting her. Curiously, she kept her gaze fixed on the woman and failed to spot a passing waiter carrying a glass of red wine. She bumped into him, causing the wine to tumble off his tray and splash everywhere.

"Fuck," she muttered and winced when she saw the big, red stain on her white shirt. "I'm sorry, it was my fault. I was distracted." She noted the waiter's shirt was covered in red stains, too. "I'm so sorry."

"No need to apologize," he said politely, wiping his neck with a napkin. "I have another shirt in the back, so don't worry. Wait here, and I'll get you something to clean that stain with."

Ally sat in the nearest nook and inspected the damage. She didn't have a change of clothes in her hand luggage and doubted the stain would come out.

"Thank you," she said when the waiter returned with a wet cloth. She was about to start rubbing it over her chest when someone put a hand on her shoulder.

"Don't." It was the woman from the bar. "You should put salt on your shirt instead. It will soak up the stain." She picked up the salt from the table and handed it to Ally. "It's best to take the shirt off and sprinkle the salt over it."

Ally arched a brow as she looked up at the woman. "Are you sure?"

"Yeah. I promise it works."

"If you say so..." Ally started unbuttoning her shirt, then remembered she was only wearing a bra underneath. "I can't," she said with a goofy grin. "I'll be near naked if I take it off."

"That wouldn't be so bad," the woman said, her eyes sparkling with mischief.

No idea how to reply, Ally laughed nervously while she let her comment sink in. *Is she flirting with me?* It was a strange thing to say.

"Seriously. It's a nice shirt. It's a waste if it gets ruined."

The woman pointed to Ally's trench coat. "Why don't you put that on? I'm sure the flight attendant can get you a pajama top from first class to wear on the flight. They'll have spares."

"Okay. That's a good idea." Ally contemplated going to the restrooms but decided her seating nook was private enough for a quick change. She grabbed her coat, turned around, and swiftly swapped her shirt for her coat. "I look like a flasher now, don't I?" she said sheepishly, tying it firmly at the waist.

The woman laughed. "I wouldn't run away if I saw you standing behind a tree."

There it was again. Another comment that could very well pass for flirtatious. Before Ally could reply, the woman had grabbed her shirt, draped it over the coffee table, and emptied the salt dispenser over the stain.

"There you go. That should work miracles if you leave it for a while. The rest will come off in the wash." She smiled. "And now that I've seen you in your underwear, I might as well introduce myself. I'm Candice Blackwater."

"Ally Brenner," Ally said. "Thank you so much for your help." Part of her was intrigued by Candice's strange comments. Was she giving off gay vibes today? Ally wanted to clear the air, but randomly announcing she was straight seemed like an awkward thing to do, so she let it go and pointed to the chair next to hers. "Want to join me? I'd buy you a drink but it's free here. I can get you one, though."

"I'm good. I already have a martini, but yes, I'd love to join you." Candice sat, stretched her legs in front of her, and sipped her drink. "Mm...I needed this. It's been a long day," she said with a sigh.

"Did you come straight from the office?" Ally asked.

"No. I worked from my mom's house today, but I started

Chance Encounters

at six this morning and I haven't had a break." Candice checked her watch. "I like long-haul night flights. They're an excuse to relax. Don't you think?"

"It is now. I was lucky to get upgraded."

"Oh, good for you." Candice raised her glass in a toast. "I'm off to Amsterdam. What about you?"

"Me too. What takes you there?" Ally asked. "Let me guess. You're in the laundry business?"

"I wish. That would be blissfully straightforward and stress-free. No, I'm a private investor. I got lucky in the property market, which enabled me to move on to bigger commercial builds. I only focus on the financials, though. I don't get involved in design or build, but I found that the Netherlands is a fruitful market, so I relocated there."

"Interesting." Ally regarded Candice. Despite her no-nonsense dress sense, there was something playful about her. "Are you based in Amsterdam?"

"Yes, but I'm Canadian. I fly back and forth regularly. I have investments in Vancouver, and my family is there. Do you live in Amsterdam?"

"No, I live in Vancouver. I run a project management company together with a friend, and I'm pitching for a job in Amsterdam tomorrow. It's for a huge warehouse conversion."

"So, we're in the same kind of business," Candice concluded.

"Yes, albeit at opposite ends. You hold the reins, I'm just the workhorse," Ally joked. "We're in the final stage of the selection process, so one of us has to be there in person."

"Cool. Are you nervous?"

"Yes," Ally admitted. "I'm terrified."

"I can't tell from looking at you. You have a calm presence." Candice shot Ally a smile over the rim of her martini glass. "Are you prepared? Do you have a clean shirt with you?"

"Always." Ally laughed. "I'm totally OCD when it comes to pitching, and I packed ten decent outfits, which is ridiculous since I'm only there for two nights."

"That's a shame. Amsterdam is a beautiful city. Will it be your first visit?"

"Yes, but we're busy wrapping up a job here, so I couldn't spare more time." Ally narrowed her eyes at Candice. "You look familiar. Have we met before?"

"I don't think so." Candice looked away for a beat. "But perhaps we've crossed paths in Vancouver?"

"Hmm..." For some reason, Ally wasn't sure she believed her. She was good at reading people, and she had a feeling Candice was lying. Not that it mattered; Candice was just a fellow passenger, and it was unlikely they'd ever see each other again. "Well, I'm glad we met now," she finally said, pointing to her shirt. The salt had soaked up some of the wine, and the red stain was fading. "It looks like you saved my shirt."

2

ALLY

Ally was greeted by the sight of plush leather seats bathed in soft, ambient lighting. The spacious cabin exuded an aura of refinement, with modern decor and clean lines adding to the sense of elegance. She sank into her seat's embrace and made herself comfortable while the flight attendant searched for the pajama top she'd requested. She kept an eye out for Candice, who had left for the restrooms just as they were about to board. With only forty business-class seats, she couldn't be far away.

Staring out of the window, healthy nerves swirled in her core. It was finally happening. The chance to land a big, international client and grow their company was so close she could almost taste it. Ally and Dan had worked very hard in the past years, but if they won the pitch, every single all-nighter would be worth it. They'd started working for small companies, spreading their focus over sometimes twelve projects at once. It wasn't until they changed their strategy and took on fewer but bigger clients that things started to shift for them. They'd built a credible portfolio and got noticed by the industry now.

"No way." Candice's voice pulled her out of her thoughts. "Hello again. Is this really your seat?" She held up her ticket. "I'm in 3b. I'm next to you."

"Oh. What are the odds?" Ally lowered the screen between them so they could see each other better. "Let me know if you want privacy. I won't take it personally."

Candice laughed. "I normally keep to myself on flights, but I'll admit, I'm delighted to have you as my neighbor." She smiled at a flight attendant offering them a glass of Champagne and passed one to Ally. "Cheers," she said. "To new friends."

"To new friends." Ally returned her smile and took a sip, cursing herself for not making more of an effort with her appearance. Her long, dark hair was pulled into a messy ponytail, and she hadn't bothered with makeup. On top of that, she was wrapped in her trench coat and waiting for a pajama top that would no doubt be far from charming. "Can you sleep on flights?" she asked, pulling the elastic band out of her hair and shaking it loose.

"No. But that's okay. I always look forward to doing nothing, so I don't mind. Can you sleep?"

"Never," Ally said. "It's been a while since I've been on a long-haul flight, though. Traveling has been thin on the ground since Dan—he's my business partner—and I started our company. Most of our clients are in Vancouver." A funny, nervous flutter ran through her core as she met Candice's eyes. It was a strange and unexpected sensation, and she swiftly turned her gaze to her screen. "I like to watch movies on flights. I tend to fall asleep easily at home, so I rarely make it until the end."

"My guilty pleasure on flights is sudoku, crosswords, and gossip magazines." Candice pointed to the shopping bag on the floor between her feet. "But I like movies too." She tilted her head. "Are you married? Boyfriend? Girlfriend?"

"No husband or boyfriend," Ally said, ensuring there was no question about her sexuality. "I'm single."

Candice bit her lip and shot Ally a look that caused another flutter. "Same here. Single."

Focusing on her Champagne, Ally wondered what caused her to react to Candice in such a physical manner. "Are you... Are you gay?" she finally asked, then waved a hand. "I'm sorry. Was that too personal of a question?"

"Not at all." Candice laughed. "Do you get that vibe from me?"

"Yes," Ally admitted. "Not that I care," she hastily added. "It was just my first impression."

"Well, you're right. I'm forty-one, very, very gay, and I've been single for four years. I have fun, but I rarely meet someone I click with." Candice finished her drink and put her glass to the side. "How long have you been single?"

"A little over two years. My ex-partner moved to Paris for work." Ally paused, deciding on how much to share. "Long-distance didn't work out for us," she finally said.

"Have you dated since?"

Ally shook her head and let out a sarcastic chuckle. "No. I'm done with drama. I just want to focus on my career."

"Fair enough. Personally, I never seem to have time to focus on dating," Candice said. "But I won't lie, I miss intimacy." The corners of her mouth tugged up. "I miss sex."

"Yeah." Ally chuckled, and a blush rose to her cheeks. "It's been a while." A silence fell between them, and she was glad the flight attendant arrived with her pajama top.

"Here you go, Miss Brenner. It's probably too big for you, but it was the only women's size we had left." She pointed to their glasses. "Would you like me to refill your glasses before takeoff?"

"Sure." Ally felt nervous and a little anxious, but by now, it had nothing to do with her upcoming pitch and everything to do with her neighbor.

Candice put up her aisle screen, shielding them from the other rows of seats. "Go ahead. It's nothing I haven't already seen," she joked. She turned away, waited for Ally to get changed, and turned back when Ally handed her trench coat to the flight attendant to stow away. "That's better."

"Much better." Ally was aware of Candice's eyes lowering to the swell of her breasts. The simple navy top was soft and comfortable but way too big for her. It was hanging off one shoulder, and the V-neck barely covered her bra.

"I like the neckline," Candice said, arching a brow. She had the kind of boyish smirk only overly confident people could pull off.

Ally shook her head and rolled her eyes. "Okay, I have to ask. Are you flirting with me?"

"Uh-huh." There it was. The cocky confidence of a woman who was used to getting what she wanted. "Do you mind?"

Ally's pulse raced as she stared at Candice. This was a first, and she wasn't sure how she felt about it. It was flattering and entertaining, but Candice's unapologetic honesty also shocked her a little. "As long as you don't expect me to flirt back."

"I don't. At least, not yet."

"Not yet?"

Candice dropped a silence as she looked her over. "It's a long flight. Anything can happen."

"Anything apart from that," Ally said. "I think you have the wrong idea of me. I'm one hundred percent straight. But by all means, keep going. It's doing wonders for my ego."

3

ALLY

"*E*ver been on a romantic date with a woman?" Candice turned on the LED candles that came with the dinner service. Their tables were laid with white linen and silverware, and she'd dimmed their overhead lights.

"No." The question made Ally laugh, and she didn't dare look her in the eyes. "I'm straight," she stated again, examining her tuna tartare.

"Hmm..." Candice dug into her Arabic mezze. "This is pretty romantic, though, don't you think?"

Ally chuckled and shook her head. "Whatever it is you're trying, it won't work." She attempted to sound casual, but the flutter in her stomach kept returning each time Candice turned up the charm.

"We'll see." Candice checked her watch. "We still have seven hours."

"When was your last romantic date?" Ally asked, ignoring her advances.

"Last month. It wasn't that romantic, though. There was no chemistry. I decided to explore online dating, but that was a mistake. It's impossible to gauge if there will be chemistry when you meet someone online, so I've found it to be a waste of time."

"I've tried it too," Ally admitted. "I went on three dates with men I met online, but they were nothing like their profile suggested. One didn't even look remotely like his picture."

"That bad?"

"Yeah. He had this funny, bleached quiff and was orange from too much self-tanner. If I'd known, I wouldn't have bothered at all." Ally grinned. "His name was Tanner, which made a lot of sense when I met him in person."

Candice laughed. "At least it makes for a good story. Mine were just boring." She scooped a piece of pitta through her hummus, topped it with harissa, and held it out for Ally.

"No, I'm good," Ally said.

"Oh, come on. It's tasty. Try it."

Ally gave in and let Candice feed her the morsel, which felt oddly intimate. "You're right, it is nice." She hesitated. "Want to try mine?"

"Sure." Candice smiled as Ally scooped some tartare onto her fork and handed it to her. "Mmm..." she said, licking her lips. "Good."

Ally stared at her mouth. Did she do that on purpose? Candice licked her lips slowly like she had other things than food on her mind. She had nice lips, full and peachy, and her top lip curled up just a little. That mouth had been around Ally's fork, and she was alarmingly aware of it when she took her next bite.

"What's your favorite food?" Candice asked.

"Anything Mexican," Ally said without hesitation. "My

grandparents from my mother's side are Mexican, and my mother's a great cook."

"So that's where you got your exotic looks from. I was wondering about those dark eyes. They're gorgeous."

"Thank you." Ally suppressed a grin. She had to admit that she liked the attention, and Candice's flirty, forward manner certainly made the journey more entertaining. She hadn't been bored for a moment so far; women never flirted with her, and it was an interesting new experience. "What's your favorite food?" she asked.

"Hmm... Let me think." Candice turned to her and rested her arm on the leather divider between them. "Oysters, peaches..." She leaned in and lowered her voice. "And there's something else I love like to eat. Would you like to know what that is?"

"No need. I think I have an idea," Ally said humorously. *Jesus.* This woman was direct and wasted no time going after what she wanted. "And as I said, your efforts are wasted. I'm straight."

Candice checked her watch again. "But I still have six hours and forty minutes."

"I'll still be straight in six hours and forty minutes," Ally retorted.

"We'll see about that." Candice thanked the flight attendant, who cleared their plates, and she rubbed her hands together when their dessert arrived right after. "Yum. Chocolate mousse." A mischievous smirk played around her mouth when she glanced at Ally's plate. "Grilled peaches and mascarpone. Who's eating peaches now, huh?"

"I'm surprised you didn't order it, considering it's your favorite food. Want to swap?"

"Thanks for the offer, but I prefer watching you eat that peach."

"Of course. Why am I not surprised? It won't make me any gayer though." Ally took a bite. "Mmm..." She moaned like it was the best thing she'd ever eaten, then narrowed her eyes, pretending to analyze her state of mind. "Nope. Still straight."

"That was a sexy sound you made. Will you please do that again?"

Ally laughed. "Is there nothing else you like to talk about? Something doesn't involve sex?"

Candice shrugged. "I'm under time pressure. I can't afford to get sidetracked by chitchat about hobbies and family history."

"How about pets? Do you have pets?"

"I have a pussy."

"Seriously!" Ally widened her eyes at Candice.

"I *am* serious. I have a cat named Pussy."

"You're lying."

"I'm not. I adopted her from a shelter three years ago. She's an old girl, almost eleven now." Candice took her phone out of her purse and showed Ally the picture set to wallpaper.

"Aww. She's cute."

"See?" Candice shot her a triumphant look. "Do you have a pussy?"

"No. I don't have pets." Ally wasn't going to take the bait. "I love animals, but I'm not home much, so it wouldn't be fair. Who's looking after your Pussy?" She could barely keep a straight face as she asked the question.

"My neighbor's fourteen-year-old daughter." Candice winced. "Ouch. That sounded wrong on so many levels." She chuckled. "She hangs out in my apartment with her boyfriend and feeds Pussy when I'm away."

"Fourteen-year-olds? I bet they're up to no good."

"Tell me about it. I've hidden my liquor stash just in case." Candice tried her chocolate mousse and nodded in approval. "This is delicious. Want to try?" She scooped more onto her spoon and held it out for Ally.

"Sure." Ally used her own spoon instead and chuckled when Candice gasped.

"Hey, you're ruining the moment. I was trying to make a move."

"You're right. It's delicious," Ally teased.

Candice smiled wickedly and pointed to Ally's plate. "Okay. You've tried mine. Now, can I try your peach?"

4

ALLY

*A*lly was getting a little tipsy. She hadn't planned on drinking, but the complimentary Champagne and wine were hard to resist. It didn't matter all that much; she had a whole day and night to recover once she landed, and besides, she needed liquid courage to get through the flight with Candice sitting next to her. She felt strangely excited and tried to gather her thoughts while she was temporarily alone. On her way back from the restroom, Candice had spotted a woman she knew, and she'd been talking to her for a good twenty minutes. Ally couldn't hear what they were saying, but they laughed a lot. Was Candice flirting with the woman? Why did that idea bother her?

While her seat neighbor was focused on someone else, Ally had a chance to take her in. Candice was tall and slender, refined really, and she had a genuine smile and a lovely laugh. She was kind and respectful to the airline crew and seemed to have a knack for making people around her feel special. And now Ally got a good glimpse of it, her ass looked great. *Really? Am I checking out her ass now?* That made no sense at all. She'd never been into women; she hadn't even experimented in college.

Ally was enjoying herself more than she liked to admit, and glancing at the flight information on her screen, she saw they only had five hours left. It seemed that now she was the one counting down the hours, and that was an unexpected development. Even more curious was the physical reaction Candice's return evoked.

"I'm glad you're still awake," she said, finally scooting back into her seat.

"You sounded like you were having fun." Ally forced a smile.

"Miranda's a co-investor in a development. We've never met in person, but I recognized her from a video call, so I thought I'd say hi." Candice leaned in. "But most of all, I wanted to give you a chance to miss me." She arched a brow and locked her eyes with Ally's. "Did you?"

"Did I miss you? No." Ally's cheeks flushed at their intense eye contact, and she had no idea what to do with herself.

"That's a shame. I might have to leave for a little longer."

"No, stay." Ally was surprised by the words that escaped her lips as she reached for Candice's wrist. She glanced down at her hand, then swiftly retracted it.

"Okay, this is getting interesting." Candice looked her over and smirked. "You want me to stay?"

"Do you make a habit of hitting on women on flights?" Ally asked, answering the question with a question.

"What can I say? It kills the time, doesn't it?" Candice shook her head and laughed. "Just kidding. I don't. Maybe I would if I wasn't seated next to men all the time. I'm an opportunist and not shy of flirtation." She bit her lip and grinned. "But honestly, I've never hit on a woman on a flight before. Imagine my excitement when I saw I was sitting next to you. A beautiful, smart woman with a dazzling smile. I imagine you're a great kisser, too."

Ally broke out in a cold sweat. What was she supposed to say to that? She always had a reply ready, apart from with Candice, who made her feel nervous and self-conscious. Her eyes darted from the cabin ceiling to the floor while she frantically searched for something to say.

"Have you ever kissed a woman before?" Candice asked, clearly enjoying Ally's flustered reaction.

"No."

"Have you ever thought of kissing a woman?"

"No." Ally held her breath. "I'm—"

"I know, I know. You're straight. But your body language tells me you're enjoying this," Candice said teasingly. "Your chest is heaving, and your cheeks are pink. It's cute."

"It's just warm in the cabin." Ally tried to steady her breathing. Was it really that obvious?

"You're right. It's warm in here. They turn up the heating so passengers get sleepy. Did you know that?" Candice took off her black blazer; she was only wearing a white tank top underneath. "It's an old airline trick. When people sleep, they don't order drinks, so there's less pressure on the staff, and it keeps the costs down." She stowed her blazer in her luggage compartment and sighed. "That's better."

Ally tore her eyes away from Candice's breasts. They were small but perky in the tight top, and from what she could see, Candice wasn't wearing a bra. This was worrying. Not only had she been checking out her ass, but now she was also admiring her breasts. She had nice arms, too, Ally noticed, and she was pretty sure Candice worked out.

"Are you okay for everything?" a flight attendant asked, clearing their glasses. "Would you like another drink?"

"Could I have a red wine? Candice asked. "The Burgundy, please." She turned to Ally. "Will you join me for a glass?"

Ally hesitated, then nodded. "Sure. And a sparkling water, please." She regarded Candice. "Are you trying to get me drunk?"

"Yes," Candice said matter-of-factly. "Ticktock." She tapped her watch. "Only four and a half hours to go. I'm not too worried, though. That's still more than enough time to make out."

Ally broke out in nervous laughter. Not only because the proposal was completely absurd, but also because part of her wanted it. "Not happening."

"Maybe not yet, but I'm getting there." Candice nudged Ally. "Please tell me I'm growing on you. I'm working my ass off. I'm generally good at this, so please don't kill my confidence."

"Yes, confidence is one thing you're not short of," Ally shot back at her. Her gaze lowered to Candice's lips, and she swiftly looked away.

"Here's your wine." The flight attendant put down their drinks. "We may not pass through until breakfast service, so please press the call button if you need anything."

"Thank you." Ally noted most passengers were sleeping, but she felt wide awake. "Are you tired?" she asked, as Candice had pressed a button to raise her aisle divider again.

"Far from. I just thought some privacy might be nice."

"Oh. Would you like me to put up this privacy screen too?" Ally tapped the partition in between them.

"No." Candice leaned in and rested her chin in her palm. "I meant from the other passengers, not from you. Do *you* need privacy?"

Ally hesitated. "No," she finally said. With the lights turned off, she felt cocooned, and no one would see them unless they stood up and peered over their screen. Now that they were alone, adrenaline was rushing through her veins. Being alone with Candice frightened her, but equally, she wanted it just as bad. "I'm enjoying myself."

"Excellent. Me too." Candice held up her glass in a toast. "Cheers to chance encounters."

"Cheers." Ally managed a smile, but inside, she was all over the place. She could never have foreseen this when she left for the airport. The upgrade was a pleasant surprise, but flirting with a woman and considering more—because she was—was simply unheard of in her world.

Candice put down her glass and trailed a finger over Ally's arm. It was a bold move, intentional and suggestive. "You have goose bumps."

"I don't have goose bumps." Ally chuckled but admitted defeat when she glanced at her arm. "Okay, maybe I do. But that doesn't mean anything."

"Sure." Candice winked. "I think you like me."

"I do not."

"Oh, come on. Not even a little bit?"

Ally sighed deeply as she tilted her head from side to side. "Okay, maybe a little," she said with a small smile.

"That's better. So, can I kiss you now?"

"No!" Ally inched back and laughed when Candice leaned in closer. "Back off, woman. I'm still straight."

5

ALLY

They were watching a movie, but Ally didn't register much. Leaning in close and sharing headphones, she could feel Candice's heat against her temple and found it impossible to concentrate. Candice chuckled occasionally, clearly more immersed in the movie than Ally was. Her arm was casually draped over their partition, and her fingertips rested on Ally's thigh.

Ally checked the time. *Only three more hours to go.* She kind of regretted suggesting they watch a movie, but overwhelmed by nerves and their growing chemistry, it had seemed like a good solution an hour ago. Although she liked having an excuse to be close to Candice, she missed looking into her eyes. It was an interesting development. Candice had seduced her, and the tables were turned. Now, *she* was the one who wanted more.

"Are you enjoying it?" Candice asked, removing her earpiece while she turned to Ally. "If you're bored, we can try another one."

"No, the movie is fine. It's just that..." Ally met her gaze, and this time, she held it and didn't shy away.

"What?" Candice turned off the movie and put their headphones away. "Talk to me. What is it?"

"Nothing." Ally smiled shyly. *Are we wasting our time?* she wanted to ask, but she didn't dare. By now, she fantasized about kissing Candice, and as Candice had stated, the clock was ticking.

"I can practically see your mind churning," Candice whispered, bringing a hand to Ally's cheek.

The gentle touch struck Ally like lightning, and she leaned into Candice's touch. What was she doing? Was this really happening? "You scare me," she admitted.

"How so?" Candice's mischievous smirk was gone, her expression serious and even a little worried. "I don't mean to."

"I know. The banter and the flirtations amused me a few hours ago, but you dragged me in with your charm and..." Ally swallowed hard, wondering if she had the courage to say what she felt. She figured she had nothing to lose. It was just a flight, after all. She could always put whatever happened behind her. "I think I want to kiss you," she said in a husky voice.

"You want to kiss me?" Candice smiled and ran her thumb along Ally's lips. "I must admit that despite my efforts, I didn't expect that."

Ally's core tightened, and her muscles tensed. For a moment, she felt paralyzed. Candice's touch was featherlight, but she felt it everywhere. The tremble in her limbs, the rush to her head, and the tightness between her thighs was riveting.

Candice inched closer, curled her hand around Ally's neck, and brushed their lips together.

Ally closed her eyes as a surge of arousal took her body hostage. Candice's lips, firmer against hers now, parted slightly while her hand fisted her hair in a possessive manner that left her breathless. How was this so sexy? So incredibly arousing?

A soft moan escaped Ally as she explored Candice's lips, and instinctively, she reached out to touch her. Her arms felt soft yet firm, and the absence of a stubble on her chin was a whole new delicious sensation. Ally immersed herself in the embrace as Candice held her firmly, and when their tongues met in a sensual dance, she lost all train of thought. She tasted red wine and chocolate and inhaled the scent of Candice's perfume and her shampoo, which carried a hint of citrus. She'd never experienced this longing for more, this kind of all-consuming lust that tugged at her.

Candice pulled out of the kiss and looked at her, her eyes hazy and filled with the same desire that possessed Ally. "Are you okay?" she whispered.

"Yeah." Ally swallowed hard as her gaze flicked between Candice's lips and her eyes. "I'm just kicking myself for not giving in hours ago."

Candice shot her a lazy smile. "We still have time. Better late than never." Their eyes lingered on each other, and the sexual tension between them was thick and heavy. "Come here," she said, pulling her in for another kiss. This time, her other hand roamed over Ally's back, and Ally shivered as nails scraped over her skin.

I'm kissing a woman, she thought. *And it's perfect.* Slow and sexy yet tender, it almost felt sacred, and Ally lost herself in the kiss. It was the most sensual experience. Candice's warm, smooth skin, hungry mouth, possessive hands, and soft moans caused sensory overload, and Ally melted in her grip. She cursed the divider; she wanted to be closer and feel Candice's body against hers, but the damn thing was in the way.

"This isn't practical, is it?" Candice said with a teasing smile. She pushed Ally back into her seat, used the remote panel to recline it, then leaned over her and eased her hand under Ally's top. "But lucky for you, I'm full of solutions."

Ally gasped when Candice stroked her belly and moved up to her ribcage, biting her bottom lip while she watched Ally intently. Her heart was pounding so hard she was sure Candice could feel it, and the way she looked at her while trailing her fingers higher made her squirm. Her teasing mouth was close, almost on hers. "Why is this so good?" Ally whispered. "How do you do this?"

"It's a little thing called chemistry." Candice ran her tongue over Ally's bottom lip, then tugged it between her teeth. "I knew there was something there." Her hand slipped into Ally's bra, and Ally moaned when she felt her warm fingers on her breast, softly cupping it before applying more pressure. She didn't feel like this when men did that to her, not even close.

"You have great breasts," Candice murmured, rubbing her thumb over Ally's nipple. It was rock hard and so sensitive Ally had to cover her mouth to stifle a cry. Her reaction seemed to please Candice, as a smile tugged at the corners of her mouth. "How does that feel?"

"A-amazing." Ally could barely speak. Every nerve in her body buzzed as she raised her chest to meet Candice's touch.

"I can make you feel even better." Candice shot her a naughty look. "Will you let me?"

Ally held her breath while her mind spun. She was scared. Scared of her own fierce reaction, scared to get caught, scared of how much she liked it, how much she wanted it. She moaned when Candice moved to her other breast and massaged it. "Yes," she breathed. Perhaps the altitude was playing tricks on her mind, or maybe it was the Champagne and the wine. But she didn't think so, and there was no point playing games any longer. She wanted Candice and had no energy left to fight her desire.

Candice's eyes darkened, and she stared at her for what seemed like an eternity before she took Ally's blanket and draped it over them. "Just in case," she said with a twinkle in her eyes. She kissed her again, and Ally laced her fingers through Candice's hair and deepened the kiss. Her hair felt silky soft and smooth, and Ally didn't want to stop kissing her. *Why is this so good?* she kept thinking. *How is this possible?* She didn't consider herself sexually adventurous in any way, yet here she was, joining the mile-high club. With a woman. What would her friends say if she told them?

Her mind faded to blank when Candice unbuttoned her jeans under the blanket. *Fuck.* Part of her wanted to protest, but the kiss was too good to break, and deep down, she yearned to be touched.

"Is this okay?" Candice whispered against her lips. For someone who had been chatting her up like some cocky lothario for the past hours, she was being very attentive.

Ally nodded and pulled her back for another searing kiss. Every part of her trembled as Candice's fingers skimmed the edge of her panties and slipped inside. The vein at the base of her neck throbbed violently in anticipation as Candice's fingers skimmed the strip of hair between her thighs. Ally thought she might explode. Was this all it took? She couldn't make herself feel this way. It was so overwhelming, she would have moaned and woken up their fellow passengers if it wasn't for Candice stifling her sounds of pleasure with her mouth.

Candice's fingers skimmed lower, finding Ally so wet she gasped against her lips. "My God, Ally. You're really into this," she said, then moved her mouth to Ally's neck. She stroked Ally until she was a trembling mess, then slowly slipped two fingers inside her.

"Fuck!"

"Shh..." Candice murmured in her ear. "Be quiet."

"I can't unless you stop. I—" Ally clenched her jaw and lifted her hips. Candice fucked her slowly, deliberately, while she sucked and nibbled at her neck.

A tightness grew in Ally's core until she felt she might explode. She was already balancing on the edge, and when Candice curled her fingers and hit a spot inside her, she lost it. Powerful pulses spread like wildfire, surging through her. Reduced to a trembling mess, she couldn't move or speak or think and needed minutes to recover.

"That was hot," Candice whispered with a smug smile as she pulled out of her.

Ally didn't reply; she'd forgotten how to form a sentence. Then, suddenly, the lights in the cabin sprang on, and she straightened herself and closed her jeans.

"Ladies and gentlemen, good morning. This is your captain speaking. We are currently cruising over France and we're about two hours from descent. I'm pleased to inform you that the weather in Amsterdam is sunny with clear skies, and we anticipate a smooth landing around lunchtime. We hope you've enjoyed your flight with us thus far. Breakfast will be served shortly."

The rest of the announcement didn't register as Ally was too busy putting her chair back into position and pretending she'd been sleeping when a flight attendant peered over their screen.

"Good morning," she said with a beaming smile. "Would you like a coffee?"

"Yes, please." Ally wiped underneath her eyes in case her mascara had smudged. "With soy milk, if you have it."

She noted Candice looked a lot less flustered; she'd even tidied her hair with a few quick strokes of her hand. "A black coffee would be great, thank you."

"Okay. I'll get that for you right now." The flight attendant glanced from Candice to Ally and back. "I hope you've been comfortable so far?"

6

ALLY

"This turned out to be a pretty great flight," Candice said humorously while she sipped her coffee.

Ally stared into her cup. Candice was so trivial about it as if it was merely a bit of fun, but she was in turmoil and still hadn't regained her composure.

"Hey, are you okay?"

Ally glanced at her. "I think so."

Candice's expression turned serious. "I hope I didn't make you do anything you regret." They'd lowered their privacy screen for breakfast service and left it that way. It wasn't like they could continue what they'd started, with people walking up and down the aisle.

"No, not at all." Ally wished they were still in their dark cocoon. Everything was easier in the dark, and now reality hit her like a ton of bricks. It wasn't that she was ashamed. Being gay was not a big deal in her circles. It was the effect Candice had on her that baffled her. How she'd had the most intense orgasm of her life and how she still longed to kiss her. She couldn't stop thinking of what it would be like to touch her. "To be honest with you, I'm a little confused." She met Candice's gaze, and her stomach did somersaults. "But you seem totally cool."

"Would you believe me if I said that's just a front?"

"No." Ally fiddled with the hem of her top. "You'll forget about this in no time, but I'll have sleepless nights mulling over what the fuck happened and what this means."

"Okay." Candice shifted in her seat to face Ally. She looked hesitant as she paused. "Confession?"

"Go on."

"Promise you're not going to freak out?"

"I can't promise that," Ally said. "When people say, 'promise you won't freak out,' it usually means something unpleasant will follow."

"It's not unpleasant, just..." Candice sighed. "I used to see you in the airport lounge in Vancouver years ago. You were usually with two other people, but sometimes you were alone. I flew regularly before moving to Amsterdam, so I spent a lot of time in the lounge."

Ally frowned. "Are you serious?" She thought back to the time she traveled with Millie and Anthony, her colleagues. It seemed crazy that Candice remembered her. "You have a good memory."

"Not necessarily," Candice said. "But I remember *you*. I thought you were beautiful and you had such an infectious laugh."

"Oh..." Ally swallowed hard. This was unexpected news. "I...I don't remember you."

"Why would you? You were straight, as you've told me, like, a million times. You didn't check out women." Candice shot her a flirty smile. "I didn't spy on you or listen in on your conversations or anything like that. I just noticed you.

And then, one day, you stopped turning up, and I wondered what had happened to you."

"I quit my job."

"And I moved away and forgot all about you until I saw you at the airport today. You were talking to someone on the phone, saying you dreaded your economy flight to Amsterdam."

"Yes, I was talking to Dan, my business partner," Ally said. "I...I don't remember seeing you earlier today either."

"I was in the business check-in queue next to yours." Candice shrugged. "So, I did something a little crazy, and here comes the slightly creepy part, so I apologize in advance. When I checked in, I pointed you out to the ground stewardess and asked if I could upgrade you with my air miles. I told her I knew you and that I wanted it to be a surprise. She may have been more cautious if I were a man, I'm not sure, but she bought the story and called her colleague in economy check-in."

"You upgraded me?"

"Yeah." Candice winced. "I'm sorry. I wasn't going to tell you, but now it bothers me that I lied and pretended I'd never seen you before."

"Fuck..." Ally needed a moment to process the information. "You upgraded me so you could spend the whole flight chatting me up?"

"Yes. And again, I apologize. I know it's wrong and..." Candice shook her head. "Oh my God. I knew it. You're freaking out, aren't you?"

"A little."

"In my defense," Candice continued, "you could have put up your screen and ignored me, but you didn't."

"True. I liked talking to you, and I'll admit, I was

intrigued." Ally was still staring at Candice. "So, it wasn't all a coincidence. It was premeditated."

Candice held up her hands. "Guilty."

"Right. But why did you think I'd be interested?"

"I had no idea if you'd be interested," Candice said. "But my track record with straight women is pretty strong and—" She covered her face with her hands. "Fuck. Now I sound cocky. I promise you I'm not."

"I'm not surprised about your track record. You're quite persistent." Ally wasn't sure what to think of it, but one thing hadn't changed. She still felt insanely attracted to Candice. "I bet you've pulled a stunt like this before."

"I promise I haven't, but I get it if you don't believe me. I'm not asking you to trust me. We've only just met, and we don't know each other. Maybe I could take you out for dinner in Amsterdam to apologize?"

"Wow." Ally paused. "Like a date?"

"Yes. If you want, but you're in control this time. Pick the time, pick the place. Anything, anytime, anywhere."

Ally pushed her plate away. She wasn't hungry and needed more coffee because she couldn't think straight. She did have time for dinner, she supposed, and deep down, she wanted to see Candice again. If it were up to her body to decide, she'd take her straight to her hotel room, but it was a lot. Their night, the fact that Candice had been watching her and even remembered her, and the not-so-minor detail that Candice was a woman. "Be honest," she said. "Are you married? Because if you lied about the upgrade, you could—"

"No," Candice interrupted her. "I'm not married, and I don't have a partner. How about I cook you dinner at home? Then you can see for yourself that there's no one in my life."

"Oh, you're trying to lure me into your lair now?" Ally

joked, and she loosened up a little. She wasn't angry, just shocked. Part of her felt flattered to know Candice had gone through all that effort for a chance to talk to her. Admittedly, she liked the idea of seeing where Candice lived and maybe repeating the night in a more comfortable setting. There was so much she wanted to explore.

"As I said, we can go anywhere. But I'm a decent cook, and the view from my roof terrace is spectacular."

Ally pretended to ponder it for a while longer, even though she'd already made up her mind. "Okay," she said. "Dinner at yours. Tomorrow, after my pitch."

7

ALLY

Amsterdam's distinctive charm enveloped Ally as the car eased into the lively streets. Narrow, cobbled lanes lined with historic buildings stretched out before her like a labyrinth, each corner revealing a new facet of the city's rich tapestry.

She was sharing a taxi with Candice, who had asked the driver to take the scenic route to Ally's hotel, where they would drop her off before Candice continued to her apartment nearby. With Candice's hand resting on her knee, the journey felt surreal.

As the car wound through the meandering streets, the scenery shifted seamlessly between centuries-old architecture and modern buildings, creating a captivating juxtaposition. Quaint bridges adorned with bicycles arched gracefully over the tranquil waterways, and sidewalk cafés spilled onto the pavements. Approaching the grand thoroughfare of Keizersgracht, where her hotel was situated, the atmosphere took on a more regal air with beautiful narrowboats and magnificent townhouses lining the canal.

"My apartment is in that building," Candice said,

pointing to a brick canal house with red shutters. "It's only a five-minute walk from your hotel. I'll message you my address."

I'm going on a date with a woman, Ally thought, still dazed after a whirlwind journey. They'd exchanged numbers and agreed to meet at seven the next day. She was in a strange, new city with a woman she barely knew. They would have dinner and, very likely, sex. Would she still be up for it tomorrow? Would she still feel the same?

"If you change your mind, let me know," Candice said. "We can always meet up for a coffee instead. Whatever you're comfortable with."

Ally smiled as she met Candice's eyes. "I don't think I'll change my mind." She was worried she wouldn't be able to think of anything else until they saw each other again. What if she couldn't focus during her pitch? The taxi stopped, and she glanced up at her hotel. "This looks a lot nicer than I thought it would be. It's only a three-star, but it looks so sweet."

"It is. Good choice." Candice returned her smile. "You're welcome to stay with me, by the way, but I imagine you might need to catch up on sleep."

"Yeah. It's been quite the night." Ally shook her head and rolled her eyes. "This is madness."

"Yes," Candice agreed. She squeezed Ally's thigh. "But it's been great."

Ally nodded, wondering if she should kiss Candice or not. What were the rules? She'd never had a one-night stand. She settled on saying, "I'll see you tomorrow," and was about to get out of the car when Candice pulled her back, cupped her neck, and kissed her so passionately that Ally's toes curled. She wanted Candice, and she wanted her now, but the driver was unloading her luggage, and she needed to freshen up. They pulled back, then fell into another kiss while Candice laced her fingers through Ally's hair. It was possessive and sexy and so sensual that Ally needed a moment before leaving the car. Taking deep breaths, she briefly contemplated inviting Candice to her room, but she felt sticky and unprepared.

"Bye," she whispered, trembling all over. The searing heat of the kiss lingered on her lips as she got out without looking back.

∼

"Hi, Dan." Ally wedged her phone between her ear and shoulder as she ironed the shirt she'd wear for her pitch. "I'm just calling to check you're still okay to send me the updated deck today." She'd messaged her business partner a few minor changes to her presentation. It was nit-picking; no one would notice it apart from Ally, but she was a perfectionist and liked to be on top of every detail.

"Yes, I'm almost done," Dan said. "How was your flight? Did you manage to sleep?"

"No, I didn't sleep on the flight, but I had a nap when I arrived," Ally said with a grin. "I've spent the past hours reviewing the presentation and feel ready. It's almost eight here. I think I'll order room service and go to bed."

"Ouch. You must be exhausted."

"I'm okay." Ally put her shirt on a hanger and hung it on the wardrobe door. "Amsterdam is beautiful," she said.

"I know. I hope we get the contract." Dan had expressed his desire to move to Amsterdam even before the opportunity of the pitch came up, complaining he'd exhausted the pool of eligible men in Vancouver.

"Fingers crossed," Ally said, turning on the kettle to

make herself a tea. Wrapped in a soft robe after a long bath, she knew she'd sleep as soon as her head hit the pillow. "I'll call you right after to let you know how it went."

She hung up and opened the doors to her French balcony. The historic canal houses, their elegant facades illuminated by the soft glow of lanterns, stood sentinel along the water's edge, their reflections shimmering on the canal's surface. Beyond, the cityscape unfolded in a breathtaking panorama of lights and shadows. The spires of old churches reached skyward, their silhouettes outlined against the night sky backdrop, while the streetlights cast a warm, inviting glow upon the cobblestone streets below.

Ally took a deep breath and lost herself in memory. She was here for the biggest pitch of her career, but all she could think of was Candice. Her smile, her touch, her laugh, her confident attitude, and her flirty manner...and that moment, up in the air, when Ally was reduced to pure pleasure, etched in her mind as if it had happened only moments ago.

She rolled her shoulders and headed inside to pour hot water over a tea bag. Leaving the doors open to let the breeze in, she put her tea on the nightstand, lit a few candles, and slipped out of her robe. Ambient light flickered over the antique furnishings in the room. The walls, painted in a soothing palette of muted blues and creams, served as a canvas for the classical paintings in heavy, gilded frames. The bed, a masterpiece of craftsmanship with sturdy wooden carved pillars, was comfortable and the bedsheets crisp against her naked skin. Outside, water lapped gently against the canal banks, and through the rustle of leaves, she heard the distant toll of church bells. The sound sent her into a peaceful reverie, and she fell into a deep sleep.

8

CANDICE

"Okay, let me get this straight." Sanja, Candice's close friend and employee, raised her hand and stared at her in disbelief. "You saw that woman at the airport. The woman you were ogling in the lounge years ago, which, let's be honest, is creepy in itself. Then you listened in on her phone conversation, and when you overheard that she was heading to Amsterdam, you secretly upgraded her so she'd sit next to you." She frowned. "And then you spent the entire flight preying on her until she finally gave in. That's wrong on so many levels."

"It's not," Candice said defensively. "Ally liked that I was flirting with her. She wouldn't have kissed me if she didn't want to. And the rest," she added with a smirk.

"What? You mean you had sex?"

"We had fun." Candice shrugged. "I confessed to upgrading her and apologized for lying, so I don't see the problem. Besides, she wants to see me again. We're meeting tonight."

Sanja's eyes widened. "You lured a straight woman into

having sex with you, and she wants to see you again?" She whistled through her teeth. "You must be good."

"Would you believe me if I told you I felt a genuine connection?"

"She was probably just bored. As you said, she's straight."

"She wasn't so straight by the end of the flight, and I seriously doubt she was bored." Candice chuckled when Sanja gasped. "Oh, come on, Little Miss Perfect. "Haven't you ever done something naughty in order to get what you wanted?" When Sanja didn't answer, she continued, "I'm cooking for her tonight, and honestly, I can't wait to see her again."

"That's ridiculous. There's no way this will ever go anywhere." Sanja regarded her. "So you really like her, huh? It's been a while since you've said something like that."

"I do."

"But you don't even know her. You've just met."

Candice had no idea to reply, so she sipped her sparkling water and took in her surroundings. She usually had a beer when she and Sanja met after work, but her head was heavy from the alcohol she'd consumed during the flight, and she wanted to be fresh for tomorrow. Still, it was nice to spend a couple of hours in their favorite bar, which was located in the Red Light District on a cobblestone street, looking out over a network of quaint canals and bridges. The exterior of The Crown was adorned with ivy creeping up weathered brick walls, and a rustic sign swung lazily in the breeze, welcoming patrons with faded letters bearing the name of the bar. It was understated, just the way Candice liked it. Wooden tables and chairs were arranged haphazardly, inviting guests to linger and soak in the tranquil atmosphere. The air was filled with the lively hum of conversation, punctuated by the clinking of glasses and the occasional burst of laughter.

"You're right," she said after a while. "I don't know her, but I'd like to get to know her better." She wondered what Ally was doing and imagined her behind a desk in her hotel room, preparing for her pitch tomorrow. Or perhaps she was already in bed. International travel was exhausting; Candice felt tired herself. She'd gone to work without a minute of sleep, and now the jetlag was kicking in. "She's here for another night, so why not?"

Sanja rolled her eyes. "You'll do whatever you want, so I'll stop trying to talk sense into you. Just don't come crying to me when you're heartbroken because you got sucked into something pointless. I've never seen you like this. You're all absent and dreamy." She laughed. "Or maybe it's the jetlag. It's hard to tell the difference."

"Thanks for your concern, but I'm fine." Candice pointed to Sanja's glass. "Do you want another one? I'm going to order a double espresso."

"Yeah, why not? It's Tuesday, after all," Sanja joked. She beckoned the waiter over and added a portion of Dutch cheese to their order. "So what does she do? Why is she here?"

"Ally? She's a project manager. Her company manages commercial builds, and she's here to pitch for a job. If she gets it, it will be for a minimum of two years."

"Oh? She's moving here?"

"Maybe." Candice reminded herself not to get carried away. Even if Ally moved here, that didn't mean she was interested in Candice. And even if she was interested, that didn't mean they were compatible. She may just be a fleeting adventure to Ally, an itch she wanted to scratch before meeting the man of her dreams. Sanja had a point;

Candice was getting carried away. *Definitely the jetlag.* "What have you been up to?" she asked, changing the subject.

"Holding down the fort while you were frolicking with a straight woman at thirty-five thousand feet," Sanja said dryly. "I assume you won't be in tomorrow morning?"

"I'm not sure," Candice said with a grin. "I might be if Ally goes back to her hotel tonight."

"And if she doesn't?"

"Then I'll be all over her until she has to rush to the airport to catch her flight."

Sanja laughed. "Of course. That's unlikely, though, right? I mean, she was a little tipsy and looking for a fun way to pass the time. But now she's reflected, and I bet she'll change her mind." Her expression grew serious. "Be careful, though. Don't make the same mistake again, Candice. I don't need to remind you of the last straight woman you got involved with."

9

ALLY

"And so, ladies and gentlemen, I'm here today not only as a project manager but as your fellow visionary. This building stands for more than just steel and concrete. It's a testament to innovation, sustainability, and the power of collaboration. Together, we have the opportunity to redefine your city's skyline and leave a lasting legacy for generations to come. Urban Planners would be proud to be a part of it."

Ally's words hung in the air and mingled with the anticipation in the room. The stakeholders leaned forward, their expressions a mixture of intrigue and, if she wasn't mistaken, genuine interest. She knew she'd captured their attention, but she wouldn't get an answer today.

"Here's a hard copy for you," she said, handing out five files. "Any questions?"

"I'm sure we'll have questions after we discuss your proposal internally," the CFO of the development firm said. "But you did a great job with the pitch. I'm impressed."

The rest mumbled their agreement while flicking through the files.

"Thank you." Ally felt immensely relieved it was over. Now the nerve-wracking waiting game would start. The firm could take days, weeks, or even months to get back to her. It was all a matter of time pressure. "Then I'll leave you to it, and I hope to hear from you soon."

She blew out her cheeks as she stepped outside with her laptop under her arm. As one of the stakeholders had been stuck in traffic, they'd left her waiting for two hours, and now it was past six. She didn't have time to change before meeting Candice, which threw a wrench in the works. Her outfit was too formal for a date: a black pencil skirt, a cream-colored satin blouse, and black heels that were too high to walk in for longer than five minutes. She felt unprepared, and that made her even more nervous. She wished she could enjoy a glass of wine to help her relax, but instead, she ordered a taxi.

"I think it went well," she told Dan when she called him from the back seat. "I didn't get any challenging questions, so that's good. It will be much easier to answer them over email."

"Great. And now? Are you heading back to the hotel, or are you going out to explore the city?"

"I'm having dinner with a new friend," she said. "It might be a late one, so I think I'll ignore my phone tomorrow morning if you don't mind."

"Not at all. Go blow off some steam. You deserve it." Dan chuckled. "Don't get yourself in trouble, though. I can't rush over in a cab to save you."

"I won't." Ally laughed. Although Dan was her business partner, they were friends first and had a history of helping each other out of sticky situations. There had been the night Ally had too much vodka when she was twenty-one. Dan found her in a corner of a club, and she could barely stand, so he took her home and held her hair back while she was hunched over the toilet. And then there was the time she'd had a nasty fight with her ex. She'd stayed with Dan for a week before she decided to go back to him. "Dan?"

"Yes?"

Ally hesitated. She wanted to tell Dan about Candice, but something held her back. Why couldn't she tell him? Out of all her friends, he would understand. She swallowed hard as she tried to muster the courage, but no words came out.

"What?" Dan paused. "Are you okay?"

"Yeah, I'm fine. Never mind," she said, changing her mind. "I forgot what I was going to tell you. I'll let you know when it comes back to me."

Ally was shaking after she'd hung up. She'd almost told him. Almost. Dan wouldn't judge her, but it was all so fresh that she needed to get her thoughts straight before she could even begin to express them.

She asked the taxi driver to make a stop at a liquor store and felt overwhelmed as she stared at the shelves. There was so much choice. What did Candice like? She remembered she'd ordered red wine on the flight, but it was all a bit of a blur, and she had no idea what red wine to choose. She was usually a quick decision-maker, but now she was overanalyzing everything. She was insecure about her outfit, what wine to choose, what to do when she arrived—should she kiss Candice or hug her?

"Special occasion?" the store clerk asked. She was young, way too young to know much about wine, Ally suspected.

"Ehm, yes, I suppose so." Ally stared at her. "I need something for a date. Nothing pretentious. Just a really nice red."

"Okay." The girl smiled. "Man or woman?"

"What?" Ally frowned.

"Your date. Is it with a man or a woman? Men and women tend to like different wines. Our palettes are usually more refined," she said, bringing a hand to her chest.

Ally was surprised at the question. Even in Canada, they weren't so open-minded as to assume a date could be of the same-sex kind. "A woman," she stammered.

"Okay. What will you be eating?"

"I have no idea," Ally admitted.

"Let's see." The girl glanced over the middle shelves. "You'll want something at the top end of the mid-price range, and for a date..." she mused, her fingers tracing the labels, "you'll want a wine that speaks volumes without overwhelming the senses." Her gaze settled on a bottle nestled among its peers. "This is a Tempranillo from the Rioja region of Spain. It's unassuming yet complex, with notes of ripe red fruits and a subtle hint of vanilla. It's versatile enough to complement a range of dishes, so you'll be safe with this one."

"Okay, I'll take it," Ally said, reminding herself not to judge people on their looks. Again, the girl had taken her by surprise. "You've been very helpful."

"It's good, trust me." The girl took Ally's credit card and bagged the wine. "They sell flowers next door. They have lovely lilies."

"Flowers?"

"Yes. It's a date, right?"

Ally nodded. "Do women bring flowers to dates?" She rolled her eyes in embarrassment. "I'm sorry. This is new to me, and you seem more clued in than I am, so please help me out."

"What do you mean? You've never been on a date with a

woman?" The girl clapped her hands in excitement when Ally shook her head. "It's your first time? That's so cool. Don't get nervous. It will be fine."

"Too late for that. I'm already a bundle of nerves." Ally chuckled. "So, you think I should get lilies?"

"Yes. Lilies, roses, or tulips. But roses might be too much for a first date, and tulips don't last very long, so I'd say go with the lilies."

10

CANDICE

Candice left work early and thought she had plenty of time, but after showering, prepping the food, tidying her apartment, and setting the table, she was cutting it short. Glancing at her watch, she noted she had just under an hour before Ally would arrive. She rarely got nervous with women, but she was stressing about the smallest of things. Did her hair look okay? Was she dressed too casually? Should she light more candles, or had she already made too big of a deal out of it? Would Ally even show up? She hadn't heard from her today.

She checked her phone. There was no cancellation message, so she headed to the bathroom to wash her hands and studied herself in the mirror. She wasn't unhappy with how she looked, but after years of working long hours combined with extensive travel, her age was showing. Forty-two. She didn't mind the fine lines around her eyes; they gave her character and reflected her upbeat personality. But the few gray hairs that had started sprouting bothered her, and she leaned in closer to pull them out.

Ally was in her late thirties, but she looked younger than

her age. Despite her intelligence and grounded demeanor, there was something slightly naïve about her, and she radiated a cute sense of curiosity that Candice found adorable. That inquisitive look washed over her face each time Candice flirted with her or when she found herself doing something out of character.

Candice's phone rang, pulling her out of her thoughts. It was her mother.

"Hi, Mom," she said, combing a hand through her hair. "I'm sorry I didn't call you after I landed. It's been nonstop since I got back." That was a lie; she'd been daydreaming pretty much constantly, but her mother didn't need to know that.

"Honey, you're working too hard. What did I tell you? You need to give yourself a break, especially after traveling. Your body needs to recover."

"I've recovered. I'm fine, I promise."

Her mother was silent for a moment. "Very well. As long as you take care of yourself. How was your flight?"

"It was great," Candice said, sounding way more enthusiastic than she meant to. "Listen, I'd love to chat, but can I call you back tomorrow? Someone's coming over for dinner, and I still need to make a salad."

"Of course. Who's coming for dinner? Is it a woman?"

Candice laughed. "Yes, it's a woman. Stop being so nosey. She's just a friend."

"Oh. Sanja?"

"No, a new friend. Her name is Ally. I met her on the flight. She's from Vancouver."

"How wonderful. And is she of your persuasion?"

Candice rolled her eyes. There was no stopping her mother once she wanted to get to the bottom of something. "No, she's not gay."

"But you sound excited."

"I'm looking forward to it," Candice admitted.

"Right." Her mother paused. "Will you please be careful?"

"What do you mean by that?" She knew exactly what her mother was referring to and tried to contain her irritation. First Sanja, now her mom. She hated it when people brought up her ex. It was a grim reminder of her lack of judgment. "Ally's just a friend," she said again. "I won't make the same mistake."

"I know, I'm sorry."

Blowing out her cheeks, Candice forced away painful memories. She would have done anything for Alex. They had a home, a life, and they had love. At least, Candice thought they did. But there was one thing she couldn't give her, and that had caused their marriage to crumble. She'd never talked about her ex. When people inquired, she brushed it off as something "in the past," but it still hurt.

"I have to go now, Mom," she said, softening her tone. "I'll call you tomorrow, okay?"

"Okay, honey. Have fun."

Candice felt a little guilty for hanging up on her mother, but she didn't want to discuss something irrelevant when she wasn't even sure she could class this as a date. She'd offered to cook for Ally as a matter of apology, not to get her in bed. But, of course, that was exactly what she wanted. To have more of Ally and explore all of her. Why was she such a sucker for straight women? Was she trying to prove something? That she could turn them? For good this time? It didn't matter, she decided. It was just a night. *One more night.*

11

ALLY

"They're beautiful." Candice took the lilies and let Ally in. "Thank you." She kissed Ally's cheek. "You look..." She bit her lip and grinned. "You look sexy as hell. Did you come straight from your meeting, or did you put on those heels for me?"

"I came straight here, but I'm glad you like them." Ally smiled shyly and touched her cheek where Candice's lips had been as she followed her inside the spacious open-plan apartment. It was gorgeous, with original wooden beams and brickwork. The contrast with Candice's modern furniture was striking and flowed in all the right ways. Working on newbuild rather than restoration, Ally didn't often get to see old buildings inside, and she took in the space with great appreciation. It suited Candice, she decided. Her home was no-nonsense, much like her, but it also had a timeless charm and the perfect mixture of masculine and feminine energy. There were no trinkets; each item served its purpose.

"You have an amazing apartment." Ally handed her the bottle of wine.

"Thank you. It's been interesting, moving here. All the walls and floors are crooked, as the foundation is slowly sinking into the canal, so it took some work to make the floor look level. Even now, if I put this bottle down on its side, it would roll straight toward the window. Which I'm not going to do, by the way. Can I pour you a glass? I also have white, rosé, Champagne, gin, coffee, and tea. Anything you want."

"Red is fine." Ally cleared her throat as she looked Candice up and down. She was wearing jeans and a simple white T-shirt. Again, there was no sign of a bra, and that made her pulse race. "Did you work today?" she asked, grasping for small talk while Candice arranged the flowers into a vase. Simply seeing her moving around and doing mundane things in the kitchen was a turn-on. Nothing had changed. If anything, her physical reaction to Candice was even stronger now, and she liked being in her personal space.

"Yeah. It's been a busy day with lots of catching up," she said. "How did your pitch go?"

"Good, I think." Ally shrugged. "It's always hard to tell, but I don't think I could have done anything different to improve it."

"Excellent. Then we should celebrate." Candice poured them wine and laughed when a black-and-white cat jumped onto the kitchen island and almost knocked over her glass. "Hey, girl. I told you not to jump. It's bad for your old joints." She stroked the cat. "Ally, this is Pussy. Pussy, this is Ally."

Ally stroked the cat and scratched her behind her ears. "She's adorable."

"Yeah. I love her. She was so happy I was back. She spent the whole night sleeping in the crook of my neck."

"She sleeps in your bed?"

Chance Encounters

"Sometimes, but especially when I've been away." Candice held up her glass in a toast. "Here's to your pitch, and who knows? You might move to Amsterdam."

"Cheers." Ally clinked her glass against Candice's and held her gaze. The woman's eyes made her queasy each time she looked into them. She was all over the place, restless and nervous. "What are you cooking?" she asked, inhaling the delicious aroma from the oven.

"I made lasagna. I heard you say you had no allergies when you ordered on the flight, so I figured this would be safe enough. "You also said you like sweet stuff, so guess what?" Candice arched a brow. "We're having peaches for dessert."

"Peaches?" The suggestive undertone in Candice's voice had not gone unnoticed, and Ally squeezed her legs together as she steadied herself against the kitchen island. Why hadn't Candice kissed her yet? Was she being polite? Was she waiting for Ally to make the first move?

"Yes. You'll love it. Anyway," Candice continued, "dinner is ready. Shall we?"

"Sure." Ally was hungry but didn't think she'd be able to eat much as her stomach kept doing flips. "Can I help with anything?"

Candice handed her a bowl of salad and pointed to the cast-iron spiral staircase in the far corner of the room. "You can take this and your wine up to the roof terrace. I already set the table. I'll be right behind you."

Ally was impressed as she stepped onto the terrace that spanned half the roof and took in the outdoor space. Candice had clearly gone to great lengths setting the table with white linen, beautiful, simple China, and silverware. There were candles in modern, white candelabras, and next to the table, a firepit was burning. A few big plants stood around a seating area with a cushioned couch, two matching chairs, and a coffee table. It was sleek and elegant, but the view was what stunned her the most. She could see far and wide over the canals, the neighborhood, and the city beyond. It was wonderful to be in a city with very few skyscrapers, where most buildings dated back hundreds of years.

"It's great, right?" Candice said as she joined her and placed a tray with steaming hot lasagna on the table. I never get tired of this view." She winked. "If you moved here, you could enjoy this every summer. There are some fantastic rentals in Amsterdam."

"I don't want to get ahead of myself."

"Nothing wrong with wishful thinking. Or manifesting, as they call it." Candice pulled out a chair for Ally and sat opposite her.

"Is that what you're into?" Ally asked. "Manifesting? Because if you are, you've certainly manifested a beautiful life for yourself."

Canice laughed and shook her head. "No. This is all hard work. I failed a few times, but I got back on my feet. It took me years to build a healthy business."

"Are you happy?" Ally asked. "Are you where you want to be in life?"

Candice sighed as she plated a portion of lasagna for Ally. "That's a deep question. I suppose I'm happy. I like my job, I like where I live, and I have good friends..."

Ally detected a hint of hesitation in her voice. "But?"

Candice shrugged. "Love is the only thing missing. I'm not looking for it, but it would be nice."

Ally regarded her. "I can't see you having trouble finding a partner."

"Finding a partner, no," Candice agreed. "Finding *the*

one is a different matter. I don't want to waste any more time. I've had my fun, and I'd like to settle down with someone."

"Wouldn't you class this as a waste of time?" Ally asked. "A date with a straight woman?"

"Probably." Candice grinned sheepishly. "Is it?"

"I don't know. I don't know anything right now."

"That's okay." Candice twirled her wine around in her glass as she met Ally's gaze. It was something she did when she was deep in thought. Ally had noticed it on the flight, and she recognized some of her other mannerisms—the way she narrowed her eyes when Ally spoke as if what she had to say mattered and running a hand through her hair while she searched for words, like she was doing now. "I'm glad you're here. I've been thinking about you."

"I've thought a lot about you too."

"Still no regrets?"

"I wouldn't be here if I had regrets."

Candice nodded. "So why are you here?" Her tone wasn't challenging or accusing, just genuinely curious.

Ally took a bite of her lasagna and smiled in approval. "I'm here for the food," she joked. "This is delicious." She knew she was being childish, brushing off the question, but it was hard to voice how she felt.

"Just for the food, huh?" Candice arched a brow.

"Okay, in all seriousness," Ally said, "I'm here because I wanted to see you again. The flight felt like a dream when I woke up this morning, and I had to make sure I hadn't imagined our chemistry. I needed to know if those feelings were still there."

"Are they?"

"Yes. I have butterflies." Ally couldn't remember a time she'd been so honest. "It's driving me mad."

"Butterflies aren't so bad." Candice shot her a flirty smile. "I have them too. I rarely get them."

Ally pondered how much to share, then decided she might as well throw it all on the table. "I've never had butterflies," she said. "Not like this."

"Never?" Candice's expression turned serious. "Have you never been so attracted to someone that you thought about them all the time?"

"No."

"Huh. That's interesting."

"What do you mean?" Ally wished she could read Candice's mind. "Just tell me what you're thinking."

"Okay." Candice took a bite and chewed for longer than necessary, clearly delaying.

Was it because she'd been put on the spot and didn't want to answer? Ally was desperate to know, but she also didn't want to Candice to feel pressured and was going to tell her to forget about it when Candice swallowed and put down her fork.

"I think that's sad," she said. "You've been missing out." She reached over the table and trailed a finger over Ally's hand. "But you can still make up for lost time."

12

CANDICE

"Let's play a game," Candice said as she put the dessert down. "It's called three questions. Actually, it's called a hundred questions, but we don't have enough time for that."

"Okay." Ally chuckled. "Only if you answer them too."

"Deal." Candice leaned back with a smirk. She hadn't prepared any questions, but she could think of at least twenty on the spot. "We'll start with a question everyone has asked themselves at some point. If you could only bring three items to a desert island, what would they be?"

"Hmm..." Ally narrowed her eyes. "Yes, I've had this question before, but I don't remember what I answered." She took a bite of her peach and thought about it. "Is there a lagoon with fresh water on the desert island?"

"Sure."

"Okay, so I could bathe and drink. Will there be parrots?"

"Why not? I'll throw in a few parrots." Candice laughed. "Why?" They'd only just started, and she was already entertained by how seriously Ally was taking it.

because I could train them to talk to me so I wouldn't feel lonely," Ally said matter-of-factly. "In that case, my first item would be a hammock because I'm terrified of critters, especially spiders."

"So, a desert island would not be your first choice for a vacation."

"An island, yes. A desert island, no. And I'd take a never-ending playlist with cheesy eighties music. If I'm alone, I might as well make the most of the opportunity to dance like nobody's watching." She paused as she decided on her third item. "And last but not least, I'd take a huge supply of coconut-scented sunscreen. I love that stuff."

"A woman who knows what she wants." Candice regarded her. "So you love eighties music, you love to dance, you're scared of spiders, and you like the scent of coconut. See? This is useful." Candice smiled as she imagined Ally naked on a beach. "I'd love to see you dance."

"My dance moves are not for the world to see. I'm a terrible dancer," Ally said with a grin. "Your turn."

"Okay. I would take a pair of snorkeling goggles as I love to be in the water, and I imagine a desert island would have spectacular reefs." Candice fired away. "I'd also bring a lifetime supply of chocolate because I honestly don't think I could live without." She bent down to stroke her cat, who had joined them. "And I'd bring Pussy, of course."

"Technically, Pussy is not an item, but I'll give you that one," Ally shot back at her. "So, you like snorkeling, swimming, and being in the water, and you love chocolate and pussy."

"That's right. I can't wait to taste yours." Candice laughed when Ally almost choked on her peach. "I'm sorry, I couldn't resist."

"You're making me blush." Ally shook her head as she laughed. "I'm too innocent for such comments."

"I don't recall you being so innocent on the flight," Candice teased. "But sure, I'll behave." She held up two fingers. "Second question. What's your weirdest talent that no one would guess by looking at you?"

Ally didn't have to think long about that, and she rolled up her sleeves. "See these skinny arms? I'm a lot stronger than you think." When Candice shot her a skeptical look, she placed her elbow on the table. "Try me. Let's arm-wrestle."

"Okay, if you're determined to embarrass yourself, bring it on." Candice worked out three days a week and did heavy weightlifting. There was no way Ally could beat her.

Ally and Candice locked eyes and clasped their hands tightly together. The muscles in their arms tensed as they each sought to gain the advantage, their faces contorting with exertion. At first, it seemed as though Candice would overpower Ally effortlessly, but to her surprise, Ally held her ground and refused to yield. Candice took a deep breath and poured every ounce of her strength into the struggle, but still, Ally held firm and started to gain ground.

"You didn't expect that, did you? You didn't think I could…" Ally paused for effect, and with a triumphant smile, she slammed Candice's arm down on the table. "Beat you."

Candice was astounded as she shook her tired arm and stared at Ally. "That was impressive. You intrigue me even more now."

"What about your hidden talents?" Ally asked.

"Nothing as impressive as your strength," Candice said. "But I'm a pretty amazing bubble-gum artist."

Ally laughed. "You're making it up."

"Nope. I can make balloon animals out of bubble gum."

"I'll believe it when I see it."

"Unfortunately, I don't have any bubble gum here, so you'll have to take my word for it."

"Sure. Excuses, excuses. If I see you again, I'll make sure to have some with me."

"Deal." Candice felt a pleasant flutter at the word "again." Although Ally said it as a joke, her voice went up a notch, as if it were a question rather than a statement. "Let's move on to question three. If you could invent a holiday, what would it be, and how would we celebrate it?"

"Great question. A holiday..." Ally's eyes darted to the sky. "I would love a national pajama day. The concept is staying in bed all day and doing nothing. We'd binge-watch series, get a takeout, relax... You get the idea."

"And sex?" Candice asked.

Ally's lips pulled into a grin. "Of course. Lots of it."

"I like the sound of this holiday. But shouldn't it be called Naked Day instead of Pajama Day?"

"Well, here's the thing. If there was a small emergency and you had to leave the house for a few minutes, you couldn't do that naked, so it should be socially acceptable to do this in pajamas on Pajama Day. If you're enjoying a day off and you have to get dressed, that ruins the vibe, don't you think?"

"I couldn't agree more," Candice said. "What kind of emergencies are we talking?"

"Running out of chocolate, for example. You said you couldn't live without."

"That's fair. Or running out of batteries?"

Ally chuckled. "Do you ever think of anything other than sex?"

"Not when I'm in the company of a beautiful woman."

Candice took a bite of her peach while she looked Ally up and down. "Do you wear pajamas?" She brushed her foot against Ally's leg under the table.

Ally was blushing, but she kept her eyes fixed on Candice. "No, I sleep naked," she said. "You?"

"Naked."

"Hmm..." Ally cupped her chin in her palm and shot Candice a flirty glance.

"Care to share your naughty thoughts?" Candice asked.

Ally hesitated for a beat, then shook her head. "No. Your turn. Tell me about your favorite nonexistent holiday."

13

ALLY

"This was great. Want me to clear the plates?" Ally asked. Their conversation had been fun and flirty over dinner, and Candice's foot had brushed Ally's more than once under the table.

"Don't worry, I'll take care of it later. How about another drink on the couch?" Candice pointed to the seating area. "Or I can make a coffee if you prefer."

"No, wine is good." Ally's legs felt like Jell-O as she followed Candice across the roof terrace. It was warm and cozy by the firepit, and Candice grabbed a blanket from one of the chairs.

"Are you cold?" she asked.

Ally was far from cold; her body was aflame with anticipation, but she liked the idea of sitting under a blanket with Candice. It reminded her of their flight, and that thought brought a flash of arousal between her thighs. "A little," she lied, scooting closer when Candice lifted it.

"Then let me get you warmed up." Candice smiled mischievously as she turned to Ally and draped an arm around her. She met Ally's eyes while she played with her hair, sending shivers down Ally's spine. It was a simple thing, but it felt so intimate. Everything Candice did was either flirty or gallant. She'd pulled out her chair, poured her wine, complimented her, and even plated for her. No man had managed to come close to how she made her feel. "Can I kiss you?"

"I don't recall you asking for permission before," Ally murmured.

"That's true. I seem to remember you were the one begging me to kiss you," Candice teased, inching back each time Ally leaned in. She stayed there and stared at Ally. "God, I want you," she whispered. Her eyes were oozing desire as her face inched closer with each passing heartbeat. It was a gentle exploration at first, a tentative brush of lips.

Ally melted into her embrace, losing herself in the sensation of Candice's mouth moving against hers with more urgency. There was a hunger in the way she kissed her, a fierce longing that matched Ally's. And then, just when Ally thought she couldn't bear it any longer, Candice deepened the kiss, her tongue tracing the outline of Ally's lips with a tantalizing sweetness. Ally parted her lips with a sigh, inviting her in as the world fell away around them. She surrendered to the exquisite torture, a whirlwind of sensations that enveloped her. It felt intoxicating. The physical reaction Candice drew from her was nothing short of shocking; she felt herself getting wet, and she was throbbing. Her pulse raced, and the hairs on her arms rose when Candice stroked it.

Candice moaned, and Ally loved the sound of her pleasure. She'd been quieter on the flight, but now, nothing was holding them back. No one could see them, and no one could hear them. She let her hands roam over Candice's back and moved one around her waist to slip it under her T-shirt. She'd been fantasizing about doing this since they'd parted, and she held her breath as she moved up to find Candice's breasts.

"You're so soft," she whispered. "You feel amazing." She explored them, cupped them, massaged them, and felt Candice's nipples harden under her touch. Candice closed her eyes and pressed Ally's hand tighter against her heaving chest. She kissed her again, then hiked up Ally's skirt and lifted her onto her lap, so Ally was straddling her.

Candice's confident move slayed Ally. Being so close to her and sitting like this, with her bare legs on either side, grinding into her, was beyond arousing. She tilted her head and studied Candice, taking in her eyes, her lips, her hard nipples under the thin T-shirt, until Candice hijacked her attention and her breath as she unbuttoned Ally's blouse and opened it, revealing her black lace bra.

"Do you mind if I take this off?" Candice asked, tracing a finger along the edge of her bra.

Ally shook her head. "You can do whatever you want." She shivered when Candice unclipped it and licked her lips. The way she regarded her with such immense hunger made anticipation rage through Ally's system.

"Look at you," Candice whispered, moving Ally's bra up. She leaned in to kiss her breasts, and Ally threw her head back and moaned. Candice's tongue traced her curves, and her warm lips enveloped her nipples. "You're so, so beautiful."

Lost in the rapture of her touch, Ally's every nerve hummed with a raw, visceral energy that left her breathless and wanting more. She found it hard to believe a woman's mouth was on her breasts. As she watched Candice feast on her, she knew it was a sight she'd remember forever. The woman was ravishingly attractive, especially now, with that hazy look in her eyes. Her blonde hair was messy from having Ally's hands all over it, and her brows furrowed each time she looked up as if she was continuously surprised to see Ally's face. Her lips lowered to Ally's ribcage while strong hands steadied her from behind so she wouldn't fall back.

Longing for more, Ally pushed her back and kissed her while she tugged at the hem of Candice's shirt. "Please take this off." She needed to feel her skin. She needed all of her.

Candice glanced in the direction of her neighbor's roof terrace. Ally couldn't hear anything on the other side of the fence, but she suspected Candice was worried they might come out. "Do you mind if we go inside?" she asked. "To my bedroom? I don't want to be presumptuous, but—"

"Yes," Ally interrupted her. She got off her and straightened her shirt. "Take me your bedroom."

Candice didn't immediately get up. She leaned in and stroked the inside of Ally's leg from her knee up to her thigh, slowly, deliberately, while keeping her gaze fixed on Ally's face. Pushing up her skirt in the process, she looked so calm and composed that it almost frightened Ally. This was it. Ally held her breath. There was no going back.

14

CANDICE

"I've been dying to unzip that pencil skirt." Candice turned Ally around, buried her face in her neck from behind, and inhaled deeply. "Mmm...you smell nice," she said in a low, husky voice.

Ally shivered as Candice wrapped an arm around her waist and kissed her neck. She loved her sweet scent and the damp heat of her skin. Slowly, she pulled down the zipper of Ally's skirt. It fell, and Ally stepped out of it. Left in her heels and lingerie with her blouse open, Ally looked like a sexy vixen, but there was also a hint of insecurity in her gaze.

"I have no idea what to do," she whispered when Candice's hands roamed over her belly and her breasts.

"Don't worry." Candice slid Ally's blouse and bra off her shoulders. She turned them slightly to face the mirror on her wardrobe door, and Ally's lips parted when she saw herself. She watched Candice massage her breasts and squeeze her nipples. Then Candice's hands traveled lower and lower, teasingly skimming the edge of Ally's panties before she slipped a hand inside and cupped her sex.

Ally was so sensitive that her whole body convulsed at the contact. She moaned as her head fell back against Candice's shoulder, but Candice gently nudged her back in position.

"I want you to watch," she said. A trace of authority rang in her voice. "I want you to see what I'm doing to you, so you'll remember it." Candice suspected Ally wasn't used to being told what to do, but the expression on her face told her she liked it.

"I can't keep my eyes open if you continue to do what you're doing."

"Yes, you can." Candice's lips pulled into a mischievous smile as she met Ally's eyes in the mirror. She ran her fingers up and down and moaned at the pool of liquid desire that coated her fingers. "You're so wet. Is that for me?"

"Uh-huh," Ally said in a strangled voice. She rolled her hips and covered Candice's hands with her own. Leaning back against her, she seemed unsteady on her feet as Candice traced the contours of her body with a reverence that bordered on worship.

"Watch." Candice circled Ally's clit until she could barely stand and squeezed her nipples so hard she winced. Just as Ally was about to climax, she stopped and withdrew her hand.

"No, don't stop. I—"

"I'm not stopping. I've only just started," Candice whispered. "How about you lie down?" She walked Ally toward the bed and nudged her back into the pillows, then tugged off her panties in one smooth motion. "Finally, I have you to myself." She removed Ally's heels and dropped them on the floor. "I love these heels, but I'm afraid you might pierce my skin when your legs are wrapped around my neck," she teased, licking her lips. The sight of Ally's sex tested her patience. She wanted to devour her, but she also wanted it to last.

Ally's breath hitched, and her eyes darkened. She clearly loved the sexy talk, so Candice continued while she pushed her legs apart.

"I can't wait to taste your pussy." Lowering herself against Ally's sex, she kissed her softly and smiled as Ally's hips elevated off the mattress. Applying more pressure, she used her tongue, drawing a throaty cry from Ally's lips. She tasted sweet and sexy, like angel dust on her tongue.

"Ahhh!" Ally grasped at the sheets. "Yes!" She clenched her jaw, and a deep frown appeared between her brows. "Yes! Fuck, yes!" Then another gasp followed as her chest shot up. She shifted, buckled, and rolled in delight while her head moved from side to side.

Candice moaned as she feasted on her. She loved being Ally's first woman, and from her reaction, she doubted anyone had made her feel this way before. She was more responsive than any woman Candice had been with and reacted like each touch came as a complete shock to her system.

When Ally was about to hit a climax again, Candice pulled back to meet her eyes. "Wait."

"I can't. You're killing me."

"Yes, you can." Candice smiled as she raised herself and removed her top. "Can I undress?"

"Please. Take everything off." Ally stared at her in awe when she got up to remove her jeans and briefs. Her eyes roamed over Candice's breasts, stomach, and hips, and settled on the small patch of dark hair between her thighs. She swallowed hard.

Candice didn't move. She wanted to give Ally time to take her in and to change her mind. As exciting as this was, she imagined Ally was in turmoil, stuck somewhere between desire and fear of the unknown. "Are you okay?"

"Yes." Ally glanced over her again, then spread her arms. "Come here. I want to feel you."

Candice was throbbing as she crawled back onto the bed and steadied herself over Ally. She wedged a knee between her thighs, and Ally gasped in delight when Candice slowly lowered herself on top of her. Ally felt like a warm embrace, and she sighed as she slotted into her curves and wallowed in her closeness. She kissed her like she wanted, like the fervent need inside her demanded. Hard, with intense conviction and longing while she cupped her face and laced her fingers through her hair. Their bodies pressed together feverishly, there was a sense of homecoming in their connection, a feeling of completeness, and she sensed by Ally's tight embrace that she felt the same.

"Want to feel something amazing?" she whispered.

"I don't think it can get any better than this."

"Just wait and see." Candice used her knee to spread Ally's legs further apart and pushed into her center. Grinding her sex against Ally's clit, they both cried out at the intense sensation that threatened to consume them both. Trembling, shaking, panting, they moved languidly, their lips and bodies locked like magnets.

"Holy F—" Ally bit her lip and shut her eyes tight. "I can't wait. I'm—"

Candice pushed harder as her core tightened in a delightful buildup of rhythmic contractions. Tension and pleasure spread deeper and farther, causing a head rush. Ally moaned and dug her nails into Candice's back, pulling her in tightly. Connected on all levels, Candice felt wonderfully close to her, and still, she wanted to be closer. She lifted her head to look at Ally while they crashed together, and she was so beautiful that Candice lost herself in the gravity of the moment. Her brows were furrowed, and her jaw clenched as she stared up at Candice with a mixture of wonderment and pleasure.

Finally relaxing, Ally went limp beneath her, and Candice let out a deep sigh of delight and she buried her face in her neck. This was dangerous. Already, it was too good to give up.

15

ALLY

Ally's eyelids fluttered open, as she blinked away the remnants of sleep. The warmth of the morning enveloped her in a tender embrace, and she felt a soft weight against her side. She turned to find the source, a smile tugging at the corners of her lips as she beheld the sight of Candice nestled beside her.

The scent in the room held traces of their lingering passion, and Ally basked in the memories. Last night had changed her. Candice had changed her, and whatever happened, she knew she would remember every moment until the day she took her last breath.

With a tender touch, she reached out to brush a stray strand of hair from Candice's face, her fingers trailing caresses along the curve of her cheek. Candice stirred, and a soft sigh escaped her as she woke.

"Good morning," she said with a smile, her voice barely more than a breathless murmur as she leaned into Ally's touch.

"Good morning. I didn't mean to wake you."

Candice shifted closer, and Ally felt the warmth of her

body radiating against her. Almost mirroring Ally's actions, Candice reached out tentatively and traced the curve of Ally's jawline with her fingertips. "No, I'm glad you did. This is nice." She locked her eyes with Ally's, and Ally lost herself in the pools of deep, endless blue that shimmered in the morning light.

Their bodies molded together perfectly, limbs entangled in an embrace. Ally's hands roamed Candice's back, eliciting shivers of pleasure with every touch. She felt a little emotional. It was such a beautiful, sweet, and intimate way of waking up, and she didn't want the morning to end.

"What time is your flight?" Candice asked.

Ally glanced at the clock on the nightstand. "In five hours." She hesitated. "I wish we had more time."

"Me too. Can I take you to the airport?"

"I'd like that." Ally kissed her softly. There was so much she wanted to say, but she didn't know where to start. Her thoughts were all over the place, and she had no idea how Candice felt.

"Would you like to go somewhere before you leave?" Candice asked. "It's your first time in Amsterdam, and you haven't seen much of the city."

"Honestly, I'd rather lie here for a little longer," Ally said. "Don't you have to work, though?"

"No. I'll message them to let them know I'll be in later today. I don't want to miss out on time with you." A hint of sadness flicked across Candice's gaze as she smiled. "So, what now?"

Ally bit her lip and frowned. "Yeah...what now? Do you want more?" She laced her fingers through Candice's hair, and the strands caught the light, framing her face in a golden glow. She was so beautiful, so effortlessly attractive, especially now, in her sleepy state. There was no power suit and no cocky front. Just a fascinating woman who took Ally's breath away.

"I'd love to see you again. But I'm also conscious that you might change your mind, and we don't live around the corner from each other," Candice said. "I don't want you to feel pressured."

"I don't feel pressured. I feel happy. And a little sad that we have to say goodbye," Ally added. "It's been amazing with you. The most beautiful, exciting, and surprising forty-eight hours." She chuckled. "If someone had told me I'd end up in bed with a woman on my work trip last week, I'd have laughed, but now it makes so much sense."

"Really?" Candice's smile widened. "I'm glad to hear that."

"It's like a veil has been lifted, revealing a truth that was always there. So yes, I'd love to see you again. I don't know when or how, but if I don't get the contract, please let me know when you're next in Vancouver."

"And if you do get the contract?" Candice arched a brow.

"Then you'll be the first stop on my way from the airport," Ally said. She giggled when Candice rolled on top of her. "Seriously, I really want to stay in touch. I don't expect you to wait around until we meet again. I'm sure you have women lined up to date you, so no strings."

"If that's what you want." Candice cupped her face and lifted her head to look at Ally. "But I think you have the wrong idea of me. If someone feels right for me, I'm all in. Emotionally, mentally..." She kissed her way down Ally's breasts. "Physically..."

"Mmm..." Ally gasped when Candice sucked a nipple into her mouth and twirled her tongue around it. "I especially like the physical part." She made it sound like a joke, but she was permanently aroused around Candice, constantly craving her.

Candice looked up with a smirk and pinned Ally's hands down. "I'm giving you something to remember me by. I want you to think of me on your flight."

"Oh, I will. That's a given," Ally said, closing her eyes when Candice trailed her tongue down over her stomach. Clasping onto the sheets, she held her breath and moaned as Candice devoured her.

16

CANDICE

The bittersweet ache of their impending farewell lingered as Candice faced Ally at the airport.

"I'm not ready to go," Ally admitted, her voice cracking with emotion. "I'm sorry. I'm not normally like this. I don't know what's gotten into me. I suppose I should pull myself together. My pitch went well, which is what I came here for, but..." She paused. "But I didn't see this coming."

"It doesn't have to be the end." Candice's heart clenched at the vulnerability in Ally's eyes. The raw honesty of her words struck a chord deep within her. "I'll let you know when I'll be in Vancouver." She forced a smile. "And let me know if you get that job."

"Of course." Ally took her hand. "Whatever happens, please don't forget about me." It sounded so definite the way she said it, as if she had no desire for this to work out long-term. Perhaps she didn't.

"I won't forget," she promised. If this was it for Ally, Candice wouldn't blame her for leaving her heart in tatters. In the end, it was nothing more than a passing encounter that Candice had somewhat orchestrated with a straight woman who was now sexually confused.

Candice didn't feel smug about it. Quite the opposite. She hoped Ally would be okay and that their whirlwind romance hadn't messed with her head too much.

"I'll see you soon," she said, pulling Ally into a hug. Surprised to feel her eyes well up, Candice swallowed down the lump in her throat. This wasn't supposed to happen. Getting emotional over someone she barely knew made no sense, but their goodbye felt like a loss.

"Yeah. I'll see you soon." Ally reluctantly pulled away from her, their fingers lingering as they clung to the remnants of their fleeting connection. "Thank you and take care." She disappeared through the security gates, each step carrying them farther apart until they were nothing more than two strangers lost in the crowd.

"Goodbye," Candice whispered, staring into space. She shook her head and told herself to stop overreacting. She'd never gotten dramatic over one-night stands, and she didn't need to start now. She was probably just tired. That always made her emotional. *Coffee*, she thought, *a strong coffee should do the job*, and headed for the nearest franchise for a cappuccino.

Scrolling through her phone while she waited for her order, she saw she had a few messages from Danielle and called her.

"Hey," she said. "Sorry, I was busy."

"I figured as much. How was last night?"

"It was great." Candice smiled. "I'm at the airport. She just left."

"You took her to the airport? God, woman. You really do have it bad." Danielle paused. "Are you okay?"

"Yeah." Candice sighed. "Yeah, I'm fine. Just a bit sad. I hope I'll see her again, but then...I don't know. She might change her mind about that."

"Be careful," Danielle said.

"You sound like my mother."

"You told your mother about her?"

Candice laughed. "Not in detail. She was fishing on the phone, so I told her Ally was a friend. I think she figured me out."

"Mothers know everything, and you can't blame her. She's just looking out for you. It took you years to get over Alex and you're still dealing with the aftermath regarding your business." Danielle sighed. "But maybe I was too harsh on you. You've been guarded for so long, I'm glad you're open to love again."

"Thanks." Candice smiled sadly as she watched a loved-up couple hug each other goodbye. The woman cried as she clutched onto the man, who looked equally sad. "It's not love, though. It was a fling," she said, thinking the café opposite Departures might not be the best place to hang out when she was feeling down. "A chance encounter. That's all it was. At least for now." She narrowed her eyes, remembering a poem her grandmother used to recite.

In the quiet corners of a bustling street,
Or beneath the stars where two paths meet,
There, in the magic of a glance so sweet,
Lies the promise of a tale yet to complete.

Her late grandmother was a hopeless romantic, always looking out for signs of fate. She'd been married three times, each time convinced her latest lover was "the one." Even in the care home when she was widowed, she still managed to find love again. *"Never give up on love,"* she'd told

Candice after Alex left her. *"It's the one thing that gives life true meaning. Even if it doesn't work out, you pull yourself together and embrace it again. How else will you find happiness in this messed-up world?"*

17

ALLY

"Welcome back!" Dan pulled a chair out for Ally and beckoned her to sit with a dramatic gesture. "Coffee?"

"Oh, yes, please. To what do I owe this treatment?" Ally took off her blazer. Dan had cranked up the heating again. He always did that when she was away. The office they rented in a building in downtown Vancouver was small and stuffy. Apart from a storage and print room and a restroom, the main space held only four desks around a large drawing table that doubled as a project hub and a meeting space. Stacks of paperwork teetered precariously on the edges of the desks, and especially Dan's was buried under a mountain of files and sticky notes. The spare desks were for the freelancers and interns they hired when they needed an extra pair of hands, but today, it was just them and the receptionist they shared with the marketing company next door.

"It's been boring here by myself." Dan chuckled. "And most of all, it's been busy. I'm glad you're back." He put down two mugs of coffee and sat opposite her. "Have you heard anything yet?"

"They haven't called me. Have you had any emails in the past few hours?"

"No." Dan shrugged. "But I don't expect them to come back to us so soon."

"Yeah." Ally opened her laptop and winced as dozens of emails loaded in her inbox. They were currently working on two projects in Vancouver, both with looming deadlines. After that, they'd kept their options open, hoping to land the project in Amsterdam. Everything was riding on the outcome of her pitch; if it didn't come through, they'd have to work hard to find new clients to cover their costs. "Positive mental attitude," she said, meeting Dan's eyes over the rim of her cup. "Mm...I've missed your coffee."

"How was your dinner?"

Ally felt her cheeks flush. "It was fine," she said casually while pretending to read her emails.

"I'm only asking because there was an interesting delivery for you this morning." Dan headed to the print room and returned with a huge bouquet of red roses. "Someone's been very generous. I couldn't find a vase, so I borrowed a bucket from the janitor downstairs."

Ally's eyes widened as she stared at the roses. They were long-stemmed, and there were at least thirty of them. "They're beautiful." She turned the small card wedged in between the flowers, and her breath hitched as she read it. *Hope you got back safe. x C*

"Who is 'C'?" Dan arched a brow. "I'm sorry, but I read it. Had to check it wasn't for me." He fell back into his chair and propped his feet on the desk. "Are you sure it was a woman you had dinner with? Not some guy you met on the

Chance Encounters

flight? You can tell me if you had a hot date. Come on, we tell each other everything."

Ally hesitated, her heart racing. It had taken her a while to calm down after her whirlwind trip to Amsterdam, and now Candice had sent her flowers, and she was in turmoil all over again. The roses were a lovely gesture; she hadn't expected that. It meant Candice was holding on to her. Or perhaps she was merely thanking her for a wonderful time.

"Well?" Dan crossed his arms. "You're blushing. Cody? Collin? Carter? Chris? Charles?" He regarded her as he fired away, seemingly trying to detect some hint of a reaction from one of the names. "Chandler? Carlos? Cooper—"

"Her name is Candice," Ally interrupted.

"Candice... That's a weird name for a guy." Dan buffered for a beat while he sipped his coffee, then snorted and broke out into a coughing fit. "Wait. *Her?*"

"Yeah." His reaction didn't surprise Ally. Out of all their friends, she was the only one who never went through a "curious" phase. She patted his back and got him a glass of water. "Are you okay?"

Dan coughed some more before he managed to compose himself. "I'm fine," he said. "You just caught me off guard there. What the fuck, Ally?" A grin tugged at the corners of his mouth. "How and where did you meet?"

"On the flight."

"But you're not... You're not into women." Dan shook his head in disbelief. "Are you?"

"Maybe. It seems so." Ally shrugged. "Is that so shocking?"

"Coming from you, yes. You're, like, the straightest good girl I know. You don't fool around unless you get to know people, and by people, I mean men."

"Well, I did fool around." Part of Ally was a little enter-

89

tained. She'd always wondered if her friends considered her to be a bit boring, and it felt good to be the one acting out of character for a change. She shot him a wink and chuckled. "I even fooled around on the flight."

"Jesus." Dan continued to stare at her. "And? How was it?"

With any other man, the conversation would be highly awkward, but Dan was her best friend as well as her business partner, so Ally figured she might as well spill the beans. "It was amazing," she said, eyeing the roses. "It was a great flight, a great date, and a great night."

"Good for you, babe. If you could see your face—you're beaming! So, how did this happen?"

Ally shrugged. Looking back, it was a blur. She wished she could remember every moment, but what had stayed with her most was the way she'd felt. "Candice can be very persuasive," she said. "She spent most of the flight trying to win me over until I finally gave in."

Dan burst out into another fit of laughter. "You had a preying lesbian next to you."

"Something like that." Ally grinned. "It gets worse, though. She upgraded me behind my back, so I'd sit next to her in business class."

"Are you kidding me?" Dan slammed a hand on the table. "Now that's what I call a bold move. But you didn't give in just because of that, right?"

"Of course not. I was intrigued. Fascinated." Ally paused. "And I was curiously attracted to her, I suppose. It was flattering to have a beautiful woman flirting with me. That's never happened to me before. So, I cracked, and...let's just say, I don't regret it."

"Right..." Dan leaned in. "And now?"

"No idea," Ally said honestly. "I won't lie. I have butterflies. But she's there, and I'm here, and apart from that I'd like to see her again, I know nothing. I don't even know what it meant to her."

"It must have meant something. She sent you roses." Dan gestured toward the bouquet.

"Yeah." Ally smiled. "She did." She inhaled against one of the roses and held her breath for a few counts in an attempt to calm herself. "What should I do?"

"Thank her, of course."

"And say what? Thank you for the roses? Thank you for a lovely time? Hope to see you soon?" She paused. "I'm thinking of you? Or is that too much?"

"Since when are you insecure about basic communication?" Dan shot her a teasing smile. "My bestie has a crush on a woman. Isn't that something?"

Aware of her rosy cheeks and flustered state, Ally buried her face in her hands. "This is so embarrassing."

"There's nothing embarrassing about it. It's adorable." Dan got up and hugged her from behind. "Go on. Thank her. Just say what you want to say. Don't overthink it."

18

CANDICE

"Sorry, what did you say?" Candice messaged Ally back, then forced herself to put her phone away. She'd been glued to it all day, even at work, and Danielle was getting impatient.

"Never mind. Is that Ally again?" Danielle put down a red wine for Candice and a beer for herself, then sat back and propped her feet up on a free chair.

"Yes," Candice admitted. "I was just telling her I'm having drinks with you." Their favorite bar was packed today; they'd waited twenty minutes for a table. Mixed in with a handful of tourists were the loyal patrons who, like them, hung out here whenever the weather was good—local business owners, a few prostitutes who met up with their dogs—for some reason, most of them had pugs—and a group of musicians who enjoyed a tipple before their daily act in the cabaret place next door. It was always a wonderful, eclectic concoction of people from all walks of life.

"So you're giving her hourly updates on your whereabouts?" Danielle asked. "You were on your phone just before we left the office."

"I'm being polite." Candice smirked. Truth be told, she had messaged Ally throughout the day, but only because Ally seemed equally keen to talk to her. Their back and forth was playful and flirty, and her heart skipped a beat each time her phone lit up. "It would be rude not to reply, right?"

"You're such a sucker. Did she like the roses?"

"Yeah. I'm trying not to message her all the time, but she keeps replying and I love it." She glanced at her phone again when it pinged.

"Okay, enough. It's about me now," Danielle protested. "Me, me, me, me."

"Sorry, it's work." Candice quickly scrolled through the email, just to make sure she didn't miss anything important.

"I don't want to talk about work. We stop at five-thirty every day. That was the deal when you hired me."

"Chill out. I'm not involving you in anything," Candice said, reading the thread. It was merely an informative update from one of the companies she had shares in, and she was about to delete it when she caught sight of a familiar name. "Urban Planners," she muttered.

"What?" Danielle was sounding a little irritated now.

"Urban Planners. I've heard that name before."

Danielle checked her own phone with little interest. As Candice's right-hand woman, she was copied on all communication and knew more about the day-to-day business than Candice did. "It's from Amstel Developments. It's nothing you need to worry about. They're just informing you about the final two companies pitching for that conversion in North."

"Yeah, but..." Candice frowned as she googled the company. "Bingo. I knew I'd heard of them. It's Ally's company."

Chance Encounters

"Really?" Danielle leaned in and studied the Urban Planners website. "Is that her? She's cute."

"I know, right?" Candice smiled, her heart racing just at seeing Ally's picture. Cute was an understatement. It was a black-and-white waist-up shot of Ally in a dark, sleeveless turtleneck. Her hair was loose and curled at the edges, and she was smiling widely into the camera. Next to it was another picture of whom Candice assumed to be Ally's business partner. "What are the odds?"

"Not that small considering you have stakes in most development companies around here." Danielle shrugged. "Didn't you ask her about her pitch? Wouldn't that be something you'd talk about when you just so happen to be in the same business?"

"We didn't talk much about work." Candice chuckled. "What would be the fun in that? *We* don't talk about work, do we?"

"That's because I work for you and we're both aware of everything that goes on. It would be boring." Danielle rolled her eyes. "Well, let's hope her company gets the job so you can see her again. Maybe then you'll finally get off your phone and give me the time of day. I just got my hair done and I need you to be my wing woman." She ran a hand over her short crop and stroked her dark undercut.

"Your hair looks great," Candice said. The last thing she wanted was to chat up women, but she'd promised Danielle to help her find a date for the weekend and she couldn't back out now. "And I promise I'll get off my phone. Let me just make a quick phone call first. I know the CFO of Amstel Developments quite well. We've met at networking events a few times."

"Oh, no." Danielle waved a hand and grimaced. "No, no, no. Don't get involved. If there's one thing you should have learned from your failed marriage, it's not to mix business with your personal life."

"I'm not mixing anything. I'm not even involved with the company," Candice said innocently. "But if I can help Ally by putting in a good word for her, why not?"

19

ALLY

"Congratulations, we'd like to offer you the contract." Alfred Gould, the CFO of Amstel Developments, cleared his throat. "It was a close call with your competitor, but one of our board members spoke very highly of your company, so that sealed our decision. If you want the job, it's yours."

Ally's stomach somersaulted as she clutched her phone tightly. "Thank you so much, Mr. Gould. So, it's official?" She looked over her shoulder when the door opened. It was Dan, who had slipped out to get lunch for them.

"Yes, it's official. I suggest we discuss contracts tomorrow, and our HR department can talk you and your business partner through any matters regarding relocation and visas."

Ally pressed a hand to her mouth and took a deep breath. "That's great. We won't disappoint you." She fought to stay composed while she frantically waved at Dan and gave him a thumbs-up. "Do you mind if I ask which board member recommended us?" She didn't recall recognizing any of the people before her during the pitch, so to learn someone had personally advocated for them had come as a surprise.

"I don't see why she would mind. It was Ms. McGraw. She's a silent board member. That's why she wasn't present when you pitched. She doesn't normally get involved, but we always inform our stakeholders of the final candidates in our top-level recruitment process. She must have had a great experience working with you."

"Ms. McGraw? Oh. That's very kind of her." Ally had no idea who Ms. McGraw was. Maybe there had been a mix-up and the woman had mistaken her for someone else, but she wasn't going to ruin the victory by admitting she'd never heard of her. "So, how do we proceed?"

"You said you needed two months' notice to tie up loose ends?"

"That's right. We're just at the final stretch of two projects in Vancouver. We have freelancers who can cover for us, but we'd rather oversee everything until the end."

"No problem. Our start date is twelve weeks from now, so that works out well. Your contracts should be in your inbox soon. Let us know if you have any questions."

"Thank you, Mr. Gould. Have a great day, and we'll speak to you soon." Ally hung up and turned to Dan, who was shifting from one foot to another in anticipation.

"Is it a yes?" he asked. "Have we got it?"

"Yes!" Ally let out a shriek and flung her arms around his neck. "We've got the job!"

Dan lifted her up and spun her around. "We're moving to Amsterdam!"

Ally could hardly believe it. She'd refused to get her hopes up, and now relief washed over her like a warm, comforting blanket. They wouldn't have to worry about finding new clients or deciding whether or not to expand their team or get a new office. "We're moving to Amsterdam," she echoed.

"My Grindr pool is going to explode with cute men," Dan said with a grin. "Imagine. Handsome, tall Dutch men I've never met before. I feel like I've dated every available man in Vancouver. A whole new world of opportunities has opened up for me."

"I have no doubt you'll be living your best life." Ally laughed. "But let's not crack open the Champagne until everything is signed."

"Of course. We don't want to jinx it. So, who is Ms. McGraw? I heard you mention the name on the phone."

"I was hoping you could tell me. She was a silent board member who recommended us. Does the name ring a bell?"

Dan frowned and shook his head. "No, but maybe she got married and used to go by a different name." He did a search on his laptop and turned the screen in Ally's direction. "Nope. I don't know her. Do you?"

Ally gasped and slammed a hand in front of her mouth when she saw the picture. "Fuck," she muttered, her stomach churning. Dan's search of "Amstel Developments and McGraw" had resulted in a short biography, accompanied by a picture. It was a press photo with formal attire, a neutral background, and good lighting that deepened the blue of those familiar eyes and emphasized the charismatic smile she'd swooned over. "I know who that is," she said. "But her name is not McGraw."

"Who is she?"

"It's Candice. Candice Blackwater. At least, that's what I thought her name was." She turned away from Dan and blew out her cheeks. "Fuck."

"Candice, as in the woman you slept with?"

"Yes."

Dan shrugged. "Isn't it great that she got us the job? She must really like you."

"But I wanted us to get the contract because we were the right company for the job, not because I slept with one of their investors."

"Who cares? It was a close call. It was only down to us and one other company. It's not like they randomly hired us. We worked hard to land this project."

Ally shook her head. "You don't understand. Candice is clearly not who she said she was." She sighed. Not only had Candice given her a false name, but she had also manipulated Ally's situation for the second time. "She goes to great lengths to get what she wants." Distant alarm bells chimed in the back of her mind. They'd been there all along, she realized, but she'd brushed it off as paranoia, a fleeting shadow of doubt cast by an overactive imagination. Perhaps because the past week had seemed too good to be true. The flowers, the sweet messages... They'd messaged several times a day, and she was completely smitten. Tears stung the corners of her eyes. She felt betrayed and stupid.

"Hey, don't cry. Why are you getting so emotional? It's a good day." Dan put an arm around her. "Has it not occurred to you that she's just trying to help? That she wanted you to get the job because she likes you?" Dan said. "I mean, there's nothing wrong with that."

"She went behind my back."

"Yeah. And she did you a favor. You barely know her, so I don't understand why it's such a big deal."

"She upgraded me," Ally said. "And now, she got us this job. Why didn't she tell me she had stakes in the company? She's manipulative." She didn't blame Dan for his confusion. It sounded silly when she said it out loud, but she still felt betrayed. "She's probably married too. Why else would she go by a different name?"

"I'm sure there's a good explanation," Dan said.

"Right." Ally huffed. "I know a red flag when I see one." Ally imagined Candice with her loyal, beautiful wife, who had no idea what she got up to behind her back. There had been no pictures of another woman in Candice's apartment, but she could have taken them down before Ally arrived. Perhaps her wife lived in Vancouver. A long-distance marriage? Or maybe her wife traveled a lot, too.

"If she's married, that was a shitty move of her, but it was only a fling, right?" Dan continued when Ally remained silent. "And if she's a silent board member, you won't have to deal with her."

Ally wiped her tears and fought to compose herself. It was madness how much it hurt. She'd secretly been daydreaming of their reunion, of what it would be like to see her again, and now, nothing was what it seemed. "I feel so stupid," she said. "You must think I'm losing it, being such a mess over someone I barely know."

"I don't." Dan tightened his grip on her. "I'm sorry, I didn't realize how much she'd affected you, and I know you're super sensitive when it comes to people who lie to you. How about we get out of the office and talk over a coffee? I'll reschedule our meetings for today."

20

CANDICE

Candice messaged Ally for the fifth time. She hadn't heard from her in days and was getting worried. Ally didn't owe her anything; they weren't in a relationship, but by now, they'd gotten to the point that they messaged daily, and she was hurt that Ally was suddenly blanking her. Either that or something bad had happened. She'd tried calling her, but there was no answer. The blue ticks behind her messages told her someone had read them, though, so she sent one last message.

Ally, I don't know what's going on, but I'm really worried about you. If you've had second thoughts about us staying in contact, that's okay. I'll respect that and leave you alone, but please let me know you're okay. x C.

Candice went into the small kitchen in her office and made herself a coffee. She wasn't getting any work done staring at her phone, so she figured she might as well take a break. With only the receptionist, her assistant, and her senior accountant present, the McGraw office was quiet on Fridays, when most of her staff worked from home, and she liked catching up on emails over music and lots of coffee.

When she returned, the ticks were blue. She sighed in relief when she saw that Ally, or whoever had her phone, was typing a reply, but it stopped. *Please*, she wrote after five minutes had passed.

Finally, her phone rang. "Ally?" she said in a thin voice, her heart pounding in anticipation.

"Yeah, it's me." A hint of emotion rang through her cold tone.

"Are you okay? What's wrong?"

"I'm fine. I wish you'd stop messaging me. Isn't it clear I don't want to talk to you?"

"Okay, I'll leave you alone." Candice's hand trembled while she clutched the phone to her ear and lowered her voice so no one would hear her. "But will you please tell me why? Come on, Ally. You owe me an explanation after suddenly ghosting me."

"I owe you an explanation?" Ally snapped. "You lied to me. First on the plane. I forgave you for that because it was a cute move. But now I've found out that you lied to me about your last name, which makes me think there's a lot more you're holding back. And you never told me you were a shareholder at Amstel Developments. Why did you keep that quiet? Getting jobs by sleeping with board members is not how I roll, but now I'm stuck because my business partner is over the moon about the contract, and I can't let him down."

Candice closed her eyes and brought a hand to her forehead. Of course, Ally thought she was messing with her. It all made sense now. "Listen," she said, but Ally interrupted her.

"No, *you* listen. You seduced me, you lied to me, and now you're trying to control my life. This is what you do, isn't it?

People are just puppets in your world, and I want no part in your games."

"But I'm not—" Candice stopped herself when Ally hung up mid-sentence. "Fuck!" she cursed, slamming her phone on her desk.

"Are you okay?" Danielle asked from her desk across the office. She looked shocked. Candice rarely got emotional and never raised her voice.

"Yeah. It's nothing." The sickening feeling in her core grew. Ally had drawn her conclusions, which was fair considering their short history. Whatever had blossomed between them was over, and it was her own fault. She should have told Ally she'd recommended her, but it had seemed like such an innocent thing to do at the time that she never gave it a second thought.

Desperate to talk to Ally, Candice locked herself in the kitchen and called again.

"Will you please stop?" Ally said sharply. Then she hung up.

Steadying herself against the counter, Candice cursed. She was pretty sure Ally would block her if she kept calling, so she decided to leave her for now. Danielle was right; she shouldn't have gotten involved.

21

ALLY

"How are you feeling?" Dan patted Ally's knee and shot her a sweet smile.

"I'm okay," Ally lied. She'd felt even worse after her short exchange on the phone with Candice last week, but sitting around at home and moping wouldn't change that. "Let's just forget about the whole ordeal. You're right. I won't have to deal with Candice, and even if they only hired us because of her, that doesn't mean we're not the right company for the job." She stared out the window as the taxi stopped. She never came to this part of town. She had no business here, and it was too far to visit without reason, but in the spirit of appreciating their city before they moved away, Dan had insisted on venturing out tonight.

"That's better," he said. "Let's show them what we can do." When they got out, he hooked his arm through Ally's, and they walked toward The Drive.

"Wait. Where are you taking me?" Ally asked as she spotted the rainbow-adorned venues. The sidewalks were bustling with pedestrians, and various bars and restaurants spilled onto the street with patios and outdoor seating. "You never mentioned needing a wing woman."

"We're not here for me. We're here for you."

Ally frowned. "No. Nuh-uh. Just because I slept with a woman doesn't mean I'm ready to hit the scene."

"It's not a big deal. Just have a drink with me and enjoy yourself. Check out the ladies and take in the atmosphere." Dan gestured to his pink jeans and matching socks. "I put on my gayest outfit so no one mistakes me for your husband."

Ally laughed. No one would ever mistake Dan for straight; he generally looked more camp than a troop of glitter-coated flamingos. "Even if you weren't rocking your pink pants and that ridiculously tight shirt, I honestly wouldn't care if anyone thought we were married," she said. "I'm not looking for anything."

"Sure. Whatever you say." Dan held open the door to the first bar, and Ally hesitantly went in. It wasn't the first time she'd been to a gay bar. She visited them regularly with Dan, but it was the first time that it felt more personal.

"What are you drinking?" she asked as they headed to the polished wooden counter in the center of the room. She glanced around and noted this place was different from the ones she usually visited with Dan. Unlike in his favorite hangouts, here, most patrons were women. In one corner, a group of friends huddled together, their voices raised in animated discussion. In another, a couple shared a tender moment. They nuzzled each other, then fell into a sweet kiss. Drawn to them, Ally forced herself to look away. Seeing two women kissing had never triggered a reaction before, but it did now, and memories of Candice invaded her mind.

"I'll have whiskey and Coke," Dan said to the bartender.

"And I'll have a gin and tonic, please," Ally added. The

bartender was around her age, she guessed, and although she looked a little rough around the edges, she was quite attractive. Ally wondered if people assumed she was gay.

"Here you go." The woman put down their drinks and winked at Ally when she tipped her.

"See? You've already caught someone's attention," Dan teased.

"Shut up." Ally rolled her eyes as she joined him at a standing table. She liked it here, she decided. The dimly lit interior was alive with activity, and the walls were adorned with eclectic artwork celebrating queer culture. "Cheers to us and Amsterdam," she said, raising her tumbler. The contracts were signed, and there was no going back now. They were about to leave everything behind and face a new playground with new challenges.

"I'm excited. Are you?" Dan asked.

"I'm terrified," Ally admitted. "It's a big deal. But we'll be fine." She looked up when a group of five women came in. They'd already had a few drinks by the sound of it, and two of them glanced curiously at Ally as they walked past.

"Gay bars," Dan said matter-of-factly. "There's often a tight community, so they get excited when there's fresh blood. I bet they're already talking about you. Want to go over and say hi?"

"No, absolutely not," Ally said with a chuckle.

"But you've discovered an interest in women. Don't you want to explore that more? It's the perfect time. You're moving, so you won't have to worry about seeing them again."

Ally leaned in and met his eyes. "Look, I appreciate what you're trying to do. I know you mean well, but I have no desire to flirt with those women—or anyone for that matter."

"Because you're still hung up on Ms. Upgrade?"

"No..." Ally shook her head and sighed. "I don't know. Let's just say I'm trying very hard to forget about her."

"Hmm..." Dan cocked his head and regarded her. "Do you think that if things had been different, it could have worked out between you?"

Ally shrugged. "No idea. She's a woman, and I've never been in a relationship with a woman."

"Same-sex relationships are no different than heterosexual ones." Dan grinned. "Just better."

"Sure. Everything in your world is always better." Ally poked his chest. "Is that why your relationships have been so successful?"

"I've been saving myself for The One. The Dutch One," Dan shot back at her. "Anyway, have you gotten to the bottom of the last-name mystery? Is she really married?"

"On her website, she's listed as the co-founder along with someone called Alex McGraw. I think that says enough," Ally said. "She keeps calling me, and I don't want to talk to her, so I've muted her."

"Don't you think you should hear her out? Just because your ex was a cheating asshole doesn't mean everyone is out to betray you. He's made you paranoid."

"I'm not paranoid. I'm realistic. I should have listened to my gut in the past. There were so many red flags, and I ignored them all." Ally took a deep breath. "I'm still baffled by how stupid I was. Imagine not seeing that someone's been cheating on you for years. Not only did he have a woman on the side in France, they had a child too." Even now, years later, Ally still felt sick whenever she thought about Erik. "I won't let that happen again. Ever."

"Of course. It will never happen again, but if you keep your guard up like this, you'll never have love either."

"Whatever. It was just a fling with Candice. There's no point wasting more words on her," Ally said, but deep down, she wondered if Dan was right. Candice had triggered something she'd buried, and the pain of her past had resurfaced. Was that why she'd reacted so fiercely? Was that why she felt so emotional over something that had been so short-lived? "Let's move on from this. Can we please talk about something else?" She downed her drink. "I'm having another one. What about you?"

22

CANDICE

The crisp Canadian air greeted Candice with a refreshing chill, and she put on her blazer as she headed for the taxi stand. It was a beautiful day. The sky was a brilliant canvas of blue, streaked with wisps of white clouds, and the sun illuminated the towering mountains that loomed in the distance.

With the pulse of the city coursing through her veins, it was always good to be back. She normally headed straight for her parents' house to catch up over her mother's home-cooked food and wind down after her flight, but today, she asked the driver to take her downtown instead.

She had no urgent business here this time, and it hadn't been that long since she'd seen her parents. No, it was something else entirely that had drawn her back to Vancouver. Or, rather, someone else. For weeks, she'd tried to forget about Ally. She'd done everything to put her out of her mind, but nothing could erase the memory of their short encounter. She'd worked tirelessly around the clock and numbed her thoughts with wine at night. She'd browsed dating apps for available women to distract her, only to cancel the dates just before they were about to meet. What was so different about Ally? Why couldn't she give up? Was it worth humiliating herself by trying one more time? She blew out her cheeks as she glanced out the window.

The architecture of Vancouver was a blend of old and new, with sleek modern buildings standing side by side with historic landmarks. Glass skyscrapers glittered in the sunlight, their mirrored surfaces reflecting the surrounding skyline in a display of urban elegance. Nestled among them were quaint brick buildings and charming cobblestone streets, remnants of a bygone era that lent the city an air of timeless charm.

As the taxi neared Ally's office, Candice's palms grew clammy, and her stomach churned with nerves. She couldn't shake the feeling of uncertainty that gripped her, the fear of rejection looming like a dark cloud over her thoughts. What if Ally refused to see her? But she had to try. What was the worst thing that could happen?

"We're here." The driver turned to her. "Are you okay? You're very pale."

"Yeah, I'm fine. Just a bit carsick," Candice lied while gathering her luggage. She hadn't brought much, as she hadn't planned on staying long, but she'd scheduled a meeting during her stay so she'd feel less like a sucker for flying across the world to see a woman who wanted nothing to do with her.

Candice stood in front of the building for a moment, gathering her thoughts and summoning her courage. She ran a hand through her hair, adjusted her outfit, and took one last deep breath before heading in. She could have waited until Ally moved to Amsterdam, but she was worried her chances would lessen even more if she left it longer.

"Can I help you?" the receptionist asked, looking up from her computer screen with a polite smile.

"Yes, um, I'm..." Candice faltered, her voice trailing off as she struggled to find the right words. She had rehearsed this moment a hundred times in her mind, but now that it was here, she felt utterly unprepared. "Is Ally in?"

"Yes, do you have an appointment?"

"No, but we know each other."

"No problem. Just head through there." The receptionist pointed to a corridor filled with cardboard boxes stacked up high.

Ally was sitting behind her desk, her brow furrowed in concentration as she studied a stack of papers spread out before her. She looked up as Candice entered, and the surprise that flashed across her face was evident, her eyes widening ever so slightly as she took in Candice's presence. Her lips parted as if she was about to say something, but no words came out.

"Hi," Candice said, nervously shuffling on the spot.

Ally's body language was guarded, her posture stiff as she regarded Candice from behind her desk. "Hi." She stared at Candice like she was a ghost and swallowed hard. "It's you."

"Yeah." Candice managed a small smile. "I was hoping I could talk to you. I don't need much of your time. If you're busy, I can come back later or another day. I just want to explain a few things."

"Oh." Ally hesitated and ruffled a hand through her hair. There was a heavy tension in the air between them, a palpable sense of uncertainty that hung like a heavy curtain. "Okay," she finally said. "Grab a chair. There's no one here today. We've been packing up."

"Thank you." Candice sat opposite Ally and met her

eyes. They weren't cold like she'd expected. Ally looked more shocked than angry, and it felt strange not to hug or kiss her.

"I'm sorry. I didn't expect to see you." Ally blushed and glanced away, her eyes frantically shifting around the office as if looking for an escape. "I'm sorry about the mess. It's the move. We're getting everything into storage, and it's a hectic time. Do you want coffee?"

"No, I'm good," Candice said. She was glad Ally seemed open to seeing her; she'd had no idea what to expect after her fierce reaction on the phone. "I'm just going to jump straight in in case you change your mind. First of all, I'm very sorry I didn't tell you I recommended you to Amstel Developments. I didn't know that was the company you were pitching for until I received an email informing me of the final candidates for their next contract. It was more of a courtesy email. I have stakes in forty-nine companies, so I receive a lot of communication. I normally just skim over these emails, but I saw your company name, and I wanted to help." She shrugged. "I swear, I didn't plan it."

Ally frowned. "I thought you knew I was pitching for them."

"No. We didn't talk much about work," Candice said with a dry chuckle. "Perhaps I should have shown more interest in your job instead of trying to get you in bed." She paused. "And regarding my name... I'm divorced. I probably should have told you I've been married before, but it's not something I like to talk about. My ex-wife and I founded McGraw Investments together. I bought her out, and she has nothing to do with it anymore. I changed my name to hers when I married her. It was supposed to be a romantic gesture, but things went south, and now I'm stuck with a company that carries her name. We're in the process of changing the website and all outward-facing communication, but it's a tedious process, and it hasn't been on the top of my list."

"I see." A hint of regret washed over Ally's features. "Fuck. I'm sorry, I overreacted. I should have heard you out and—"

"Hey, it's okay," Candice interrupted her. "I'd probably draw the same conclusion."

"No, it's not okay. I have…" Ally sighed. "I have serious trust issues, and I assumed the worst." Her expression softened as her guard began to falter. There was a vulnerability in her eyes, a flicker of something raw and unfiltered that tugged at Candice's heartstrings. "You didn't deserve how I treated you." A sad smile tugged at her mouth. "And now you're here. Wow."

"I can leave," Candice said. "You're busy, and I'm in your personal space. This must be awkward for you, but I felt I owed you an explanation. Thank you for hearing me out."

Ally shook her head and shifted as if finally waking up from her stunned state. "I'm not busy. I was just finishing up." Her eyes darted to Candice's mouth. Their chemistry was still there; Candice had felt it from the moment she walked in.

"Okay. Then, can I take you out for dinner?" she asked. She felt relieved beyond belief.

Ally's smile widened as she moved her paperwork to the side. "How about I take you out instead? You don't have to be an open book. This is my issue to deal with, and you don't owe me anything. It was silly of me to get so worked up about a fling." She paused. "Maybe because it meant a whole lot more to me than just a fling."

Candice closed the distance between them and took Ally's hand. She wanted to kiss her, but she was worried the receptionist might walk in. "I'm here. I hope that shows it wasn't just a fling to me either."

Ally's eyes darted to the hallway as if she was entertaining similar thoughts. "Let's get out of here. We have a lot to catch up on."

23

ALLY

"Will your parents not mind that you canceled dinner with them?" Ally sipped her wine at her favorite Italian restaurant. Only a few minutes' walk from the office, she came here regularly with Dan and knew the owner and the staff quite well. She felt a little self-conscious and wondered if they noticed there was something romantic between her and Candice. Candice had held the door open for her, and she'd pulled out her chair. Now she was giving her that intense stare that made Ally nervous and giddy, but it was too late to head elsewhere. They'd already ordered food, and she was still too shocked by Candice's sudden appearance to devise an alternative plan.

"No, they're easy. I'll catch up with them tomorrow," Candice said. "Are you close to your parents?"

"Yes. They're divorced, and I'd say I'm probably closer to my mom, but I see my dad, too, on a regular basis. They both live in Vancouver and remarried, so I have half-brothers and sisters from their second marriages. We all get along but don't come together often." Ally grinned. "If I'm not mistaken, that's the first serious question you've asked me."

"I know. That's terrible, isn't it? Well, better late than never." Candice chuckled. "Let's cover the basics tonight."

"Good plan. So, what about you? Do you have siblings?"

"No, I'm an only child. My parents tried for years until I came along, so they spoiled me rotten."

"Is that why you always get what you want?" Ally joked, brushing her foot against Candice's under the table.

"Maybe." Candice shot her a teasing smile. "I almost missed out on you, though."

"Well, I'm glad you showed up. If you hadn't..." Ally shrugged. "We may have never seen each other again, and that would be a shame because I really like you." She met Candice's eyes as she twirled her wine around in her glass. She wished she'd dressed better this morning, but with no face-to-face meetings planned, she'd thrown on a pair of worn jeans and a sweatshirt for comfort.

"I really like you too." Candice took off her blazer and hung it over the back of her chair. Her white button-down shirt was open low enough for Ally to catch a glimpse of a black lace bra underneath, and she couldn't stop staring. God, the woman was attractive.

"I shouldn't have let you get away," she said. "But I honestly didn't think it meant as much to you, and then I thought you were married and—"

"Hey, we don't need to bring that up again. I'm just happy we're here now." Candice reached for her hand over the table. "Is this okay?" she asked. "If you're uncomfortable, I'll keep my hands away."

"No." Ally noted one of the waiters was looking at them. "It's just a little strange. I've never been on a public date with a woman, but I like it." She squeezed Candice's hand. "I need to tell you something. I don't normally talk about my ex, but I need you to understand why I am the way I am." She paused for a moment, gathering the courage to share one of the most traumatic things in her life. "I was engaged up until five years ago. His name is Erik. He's an architect, and we met through work. We started as friends, good friends, and looking back, I wasn't madly smitten with him, but I did love him. About two years into our relationship, we talked about getting married and moving in together, but then Erik got a job offer in Paris that was too lucrative to resist. At the time, I was building my company with Dan, and moving wasn't an option for me, so we decided to try a long-distance relationship in which we would fly back and forth to see each other. Before Erik left, he proposed to me, and I said yes. We didn't set a date. We wanted to figure things out as we went along. Perhaps I would decide to move to Paris after all, or maybe he would change his mind and return to Vancouver."

"Long-distance relationships are hard," Candice said.

"Yes, it was hard. I missed him, and he told me he missed me too, but we visited each other, and because we didn't share the mundane things in life such as family obligations, grocery shopping, bills, and other distractions, it was always fun, and I genuinely felt like it worked. When I visited Paris, we stayed in fancy hotels, or we'd go to the coast for a few days. When Erik came here, we'd head into the mountains for long hikes or skiing trips."

"And you were happy?"

"I believed we both were." Ally shrugged. "The arrangement allowed us to focus on our jobs, and after a few years, I brought up the subject of marriage again. He seemed fully on board but kept making excuses to move the date back."

"Right. I can see where this is heading."

"Yeah." Ally took a sip of her wine and laughed wryly. "I asked him if something was wrong, and he kept telling me that work commitments were the only thing standing in the way of setting a date. Erik was super busy, and we hadn't seen each other for about four months, so I decided to fly to Paris to surprise him. He had an apartment, but we rarely stayed there when I visited because we liked to explore France together. Anyway, I figured that if he was busy, I could work from there for a week while he was at the office. I thought it would be romantic." Ally winced as the knot in her stomach tightened. "When I showed up at his apartment, a woman opened the door. At first, it didn't even click. I assumed she was a friend, but then I saw him, and his expression said it all. That's when I knew. I've never seen him so pale."

"He was having an affair?" Candice asked softly.

"Yes. The woman didn't know about me, but the worst thing is still to come." Ally swallowed hard. "They had a two-year-old son together."

"Fuck." Candice leaned in. "That's horrible. No wonder you have trust issues."

"Yeah. I left, and I don't even remember how I got back to Vancouver. It's all a bit of a haze." Ally blew out her cheeks and leaned back. "So that's my story. I wanted you to know."

"I'm so sorry that happened to you."

"I'm just glad I found out," Ally said. "Three years and no idea whatsoever. What does that say about my sanity? My judgment? I felt foolish, and it took me years to regain my confidence. That's why I haven't dated much. I always get paranoid and find excuses not to see them again before it gets too serious." She hesitated and decided to be entirely honest. She was throwing everything on the table, so she might as well go all out. "But I also believe there's another reason I've been avoiding relationships."

"What's that?"

Ally leaned in, too, and lowered her voice. "Because I didn't know I liked women. I didn't know that until I met you." She smiled. "You opened my eyes."

24

CANDICE

Nothing could have prepared Candice for Ally's tragic story. She thought her own love life had been a clusterfuck, but this was a whole new level of messed up, and Ally's reaction made so much sense now. "Does Erik still live in France?" she asked.

"As far as I know, yes." Ally moved back when the waiter brought a board with shared appetizers. "We still have mutual friends, and they occasionally drop his name in conversations. I'm completely over him, but it scarred me."

"That's understandable." Candice regarded Ally as she helped herself to bruschetta and marinated artichokes. "I know what it feels like to be heartbroken. Not to the extent you've been through, but I've had my fair share."

"You?" Ally grinned over the rim of her glass. "The woman who always gets what she wants?" Her expression grew serious again as she tilted her head. "Care to tell me about it? Only if you want," she added. "I don't want you to feel uncomfortable."

"I don't think I could ever feel uncomfortable around you," Candice said. She meant it. Ally had a calming effect on her, and she didn't mind sharing in return. "So, as I told you, I was married." She speared her fork through a piece of artichoke and held it out for Ally.

"Are you distracting me with your story so I'll finally take the bite?"

"Yes."

"Hmm..." Ally leaned in and folded her lips around Candice's fork, then licked them sensually as she chewed. If she was trying to seduce Candice, she was most definitely succeeding. "Sorry for interrupting you," she said playfully. "Please continue."

Candice squeezed her thighs together and forced away the fantasies that took over her mind. She was about to tell Ally about the biggest mistake in her life—a mistake that still haunted her until this day—but now all she could think of was ripping Ally's clothes off and having her way with her. "Right. Where was I?"

"You were married," Ally said. "How did you meet?"

"Much like you and your ex. We worked in the same field. We were both investors. Although my capital and portfolio were significantly bigger, Alex was smart and had a real eye for opportunity. We got together a few times to discuss those opportunities over drinks, and one night, we ended up in bed together." Candice sighed. "But here's the catch."

"What?"

"Alex was straight."

"Oh." Ally inched back a little as if that surprised her. "Is that your thing? Dating straight women?"

"If you ask me if I get a kick out of converting straight women, then the answer is, no, I don't," Candice said honestly. "But have I been with mostly straight women? Yes."

"And why is that?"

Candice shrugged. "I meet more straight women, it's as simple as that. They're everywhere."

Ally chuckled. "Okay, that's fair. And do they all fall for your charms?"

"No, but it's not that hard. Most woman have a bi-curious tendency. They just don't know it." She shot Ally a flirty look. "Like you."

"I won't argue with that," Ally said humorously.

"You were a tough one to crack, though. Four hours into the flight I was about to give up, but you surprised me."

Ally laughed. "What can I say? You have a way with words. And those eyes of yours are pretty hard to resist too." She refilled their wineglasses and helped herself to a piece of bruschetta. "All joking aside, you had me from the start. I was totally charmed, entertained, and curious, so I get it. Is that how you won over your ex?"

"No, that was more of a gradual process," Candice said. "But once we got together, Alex was all in. Or at least I thought she was." She winced. "It all happened so fast. We bought a house, we got married, we started the company..."

"How fast are we talking?"

"All in the span of about a year. We should have taken our time. No, *I* should have taken my time," Candice corrected herself. "Maybe then I would have anticipated the hurdles."

"Hurdles?"

"Alex wanted kids. The natural way. It was important to her. About two years into our marriage, we looked into IVF, and it was then that I noticed a change in her. She went a little flat, and she wasn't as loving as she used to be. I put it down to work stress at the time, but later I learned that she was struggling with the idea of having kids with a woman. It wasn't something she'd given a second thought when we first got together, but deep down, all she wanted was a traditional relationship and a traditional family."

"That must have hurt," Ally said.

"Yes. I loved her, but I couldn't give her everything, and that was hard." Candice arched a brow. "It's probably for the best the IVF never worked out. She met a man and left me a few months later. They're married with kids now, so she got the dream life she always wanted." The look in Ally's eyes made Candice's stomach drop. "Please don't feel sorry for me. I'm over it."

"Do you still want kids?" Ally asked.

"I don't know. It was never my dream, it was hers. If I met someone who wanted kids now, I wouldn't be against it, but like you, I'm a lot more cautious now when it comes to serious matters."

Ally nodded. "But with me..." She hesitated. "Well, I'm straight-ish." She bit her lip, searching for words. "Okay, maybe not as straight as I thought I was, but from your perspective, you must have reservations. We've both been hurt and we've both lost our trust in partners. Realistically, we're a terrible match, aren't we?"

"Yes, and it scares the hell out of me. When I pulled that trick on you at the airport, I never thought it would be anything more than a bit of fun, but..." She crossed her arms and leaned in. "But you're special, Ally. For the first time since my divorce, I felt that amazing spark again. And that feeling was enough for me to throw caution to the wind and come here despite everything. Maybe that's foolish, but there's something special between us, don't you think? It feels like...I don't know. Like it was meant to be, somehow." Her heart pounded as she met Ally's gaze, her mind reeling with the enormity of what she had said. "I'm sorry, that was too much. I know you don't feel the same and that's okay. I just wanted you to know that you've touched me in a way no one has in a long time."

"No." Ally gave her a shy smile. "That was very honest. Thank you for that." She fell quiet for a beat. "I've thought about you every day, and I couldn't figure out why it was so hard to let go of you, no matter how much I tried. There must be a reason for that." Another silence fell between them while Ally searched for words. "And you've made me feel something I've never felt before. I didn't know this insane sense of infatuation existed, and I want to explore where it can lead."

Candice's heart swelled at Ally's words. In the quiet depths of her mind where fear and doubt held the upper hand, new roots of hope began to grow. It was equally terrifying and comforting knowing there was potential for them, and she needed a moment to let it sink in. "Does that mean you'll see me again?"

Ally grinned from ear to ear as she nodded. "I was hoping maybe you'd like to stay the night?"

25

ALLY

"Walk with me." As Ally said it, the double meaning of that simple request lingered in the air. She was still in a haze after the shock of Candice showing up and hadn't thought much further ahead than the here and now.

"Where are we going?" Candice asked.

Ally smiled as she turned to her. "Do you want to come home with me?" The night had draped itself over the city like a velvet cloak, and the route home would be quiet now that the commuting traffic had died down.

"You know I do." Candice licked her lips, and although it was clear that she wanted to kiss Ally, she didn't.

Ally's chest tightened at the sight of Candice's profile, bathed in the soft glow of the streetlights. She was restless and couldn't help but steal glances at her, drinking in the sight of her radiant smile and those piercing blue eyes. There was a constant flutter of butterflies in her core, a rush of endorphins that made her mind spin. She wanted to kiss her, touch her, bury herself in her embrace. She'd almost forgotten how good Candice smelled, and she inhaled deeply when she caught a waft of her perfume. It was fresh and clean with a woody undertone, a balanced mix of masculine and feminine notes, and it suited her.

"I used to live around here," Candice said.

"Really? In Yaletown?"

"Yes. Homer Street. I never walk this route anymore, but I used to come here a lot."

"No way." Ally stared at her. "I live in Homer Street." It was crazy to know that once their paths had been so close to crossing. Perhaps they had met and smiled at each other in a store or said hello in passing. "We may have bumped into each other before."

"Yes, it's possible." Candice hesitated. "But I think I would have recognized you from the airport lounge. I would have struck up a conversation."

"So, you really noticed me in the lounge, huh?" Ally asked. She imagined herself there years ago, talking over coffee with her colleagues while Candice was only a few feet away and she had no idea that one day, they would be a lot more than mere strangers. It was a bizarre thought. "Why didn't you approach me then?"

"I was married." Candice shrugged. "Even if I wasn't, you gave off a 'taken' vibe. Which you were," she added.

"How can you possibly tell if someone is in a relationship?"

"It's just a vibe, I can't explain it. And then when I saw you again, I was single, and I figured I had nothing to lose. I would have behaved if you'd ever given any indication that you were uncomfortable with my flirtations, but to my surprise, I detected a hint of genuine curiosity." Her grin widened. "And I was right."

Their hands met in the space between them, a tentative brush that sent a jolt of electricity through Ally's veins, and as their fingers intertwined in a silent embrace, she shivered with anticipation. There was a new lightness to her spirit, a sense of liberation in the simple act of holding Candice's hand.

Candice squeezed her hand as if she, too, had felt it. "I've missed you," she whispered, then pulled Ally across the road, away from the streetlights. She glanced around to make sure they were alone, then gently pushed Ally against a wall and cupped her face, splaying her fingers wide across Ally's cheek. "I've missed feeling you."

Tension hung in the space between them, a tantalizing prelude to the inevitable collision of lips. Ally could feel the soft brush of Candice's breath against her skin, each exhale a confession of desire. She was trembling with arousal and her limbs felt weak.

Candice's gaze flickered down to her lips, dark with longing, before returning to meet her eyes once more. She pushed herself against Ally, drawing a soft moan from her mouth. Ally's eyes flickered closed at the contact, her heart hammering as she leaned into the touch. Just feeling Candice's weight against her was enough to make her squirm in her grip. A rush of emotions flooded her senses—a heady mix of excitement, nervousness, and a strange, new sense of belonging.

"I've missed you too," she whispered against Candice's mouth, sliding her hands under her blazer. And then, with a sigh, their lips met in a tender, intoxicating kiss.

Ally lost herself in the passionate embrace as their mouths moved together in a delicate dance, melding seamlessly. She roamed her hands over Candice's back and felt her muscles tense.

Candice touched her in return, her fingers trailing through her hair and down her neck. She held her possessively and deepened the kiss as they surrendered to the raw intensity of their desire. Their tongues tangled in an embrace, exploring and devouring each other with a hunger that bordered on primal. Ally was consumed and all she wanted was more.

They reluctantly pulled apart when they heard voices in the distance, and their eyes locked in a silent exchange of longing that left them breathless and dizzy. Candice's eyes mirrored the tumultuous whirlwind of emotions that churned within Ally. "We're not far from my apartment," she said, her chest heaving as she balanced on unsteady legs.

She took Candice's hand and held it firmly as they walked the last ten minutes in silence. It felt right to hold her hand, and she cherished Candice's warmth against her side. This wasn't just some fantasy or fling anymore. Candice was here, in her world, and this felt more real than anything she'd felt before.

26

CANDICE

"Nice place." Candice took in Ally's apartment in the old redbrick building she knew all too well. She recognized the exposed brick walls, the small kitchen nook, and the brass door handles. Coming here was a trip down memory lane, as one of her friends used to live on the ground floor. She gazed through the wavy vintage glass panes, noting the cherry blossom tree in the courtyard below was just beginning to bloom.

"It's small, but it's home," Ally said. "Although not for long. Luckily, I was renting so I won't have to deal with selling it on top of everything else."

"Moving can be stressful."

"Yeah. I was hoping you could help me relieve some of my stress." Ally batted her lashes as she opened the door to her bedroom.

"It would be a pleasure. What can I do for you, Ms. Brenner?" Candice grinned as she pulled off Ally's top, and her breath caught in her throat at seeing Ally's bare skin. Their make-out session outside had fired her libido, and desire tugged deep in her belly.

"Undress," Ally whispered, her fingers trembling as she traced Candice's jawline. "I want to see you naked."

Candice's lips curled into a smile ss she fiddled with the button on Ally's jeans. Ally slid the blazer off Candice's shoulders and started unbuttoning her shirt with slow, deliberate movements. With each button undone, the tension in her gaze grew. She stepped out of her jeans, pulled off Candice's shirt, and dropped it onto the pile of garments that had gathered by their feet.

Ally looked at her through hazy eyes, then kissed her fiercely while they clumsily shed the rest of their clothes. Her hands tangled in Candice's hair as she pulled her in, their curves and contours melding into one. Finally inching away, they were face-to-face, naked and raw with desire and emotion.

Candice swallowed hard. For the first time, she felt exposed. It was like Ally's gaze pierced through the layers of her being, stripping away all pretense and exposing the raw essence of her vulnerability. Her breaths shallow and rapid, her heart thundered, drowning out all rational thought as she drank in the sight of Ally before her. Candice's body seemed wired to respond to her mere presence, every nerve ending ablaze with longing.

"You scare me," she whispered. There was a voice in her head warning her to be cautious, to guard her heart against the risk of letting someone in so deeply, because she could feel it happening.

"I'm terrified," Ally said. "But what's the alternative?"

"There is no alternative. You're my endgame." The weight of their separation melted away as Candice brushed her lips against Ally's neck, tasting the salty sweetness of her skin. Silken strands of hair caressed her cheeks and she inhaled against them. With gentle fingers, she traced the curve of Ally's throat and felt the flutter of her pulse beneath her caress.

Her head tilted to the side, Ally's fingertips sought Candice's skin, igniting shockwaves at the slightest brush of contact. Their movements, languid and fluid, grew in intensity as the electric force between them threatened to combust at the slightest provocation. It felt like a ritual, and falling into a kiss, Candice's insecurities melted away as she nudged Ally onto the bed.

She crawled over Ally and a shuddering breath escaped her as their bodies joined, her skin igniting with delicious friction. Each movement caused a kiss of heated skin on skin as Candice moved into Ally in a sensual rhythm, rolling her body while their mouths collided and Ally laced their fingers together. Entwined as a single, pulsing organism, they surrendered to the urgency.

An earthy musk of arousal filled the air between them, and their kiss became fevered and desperate as Candice spread Ally's legs with her knees and ground into her.

Ally wrapped her legs around Candice, pulling her even closer until not a sliver of space remained. The slippery friction caused their muscles to clench in desperation, and Candice felt an exquisite tension mounting deep inside her.

"I can't wait," Ally said in a strangled voice. "You're going to make me..."

Candice smiled as her throbbing ache coiled tighter. "Come with me," she whispered, her focus narrowing until she was consumed by physical sensations. With one last thrust, she tightened her grip on Ally's hands, and her knuckles turned white as they shattered into release. She held her, breathed with her, tensed with her, still humming with aftershocks.

Spent and tingling, they remained tangled, unwilling to

disturb the connection. She let go of Ally's hands and traced the contours of her face, marveling at the breathtaking intimacy they'd just shared. Words seemed inadequate, so instead, they communicated through smiles and featherlight caresses, and with their chests pressed together, the comforting cadence of Ally's heartbeat reverberated against her own. In that fragile pocket of peace, Candice felt safe.

"I trust you," Ally said, reflecting her. "I'm terrified, but I trust you."

Candice took Ally's hands in her own again. A sense of calm washed over her like a gentle tide. She had her back, and although they were scarred by their past, they'd found something healing in each other. "I meant what I said," she whispered. "You're my endgame."

EPILOGUE – 6 WEEKS LATER – ALLY

"I have good news, Ms. Brenner. I'm able to offer you an upgrade."

"Again? I—" Ally bit her lip, swallowing her words. If it really was pure luck this time, she didn't want to jinx it. "That's great," she said, still out of breath after running to the check-in desk. "I'd love an upgrade." She'd been stuck in a traffic jam on her way to the airport and worried about missing her flight. On top of that, she was exhausted from a hectic few weeks filled with deadlines, paperwork, finding a new apartment and temporary workspace, and shipping the contents of their office, so being able to rest on the flight was a blessing. Eager to have some quality time with Candice before throwing herself into their new project, she'd decided to fly out a few days before Dan, who was nowhere near finished packing up his extensive wardrobe.

Amsterdam was waiting and her new life was about to start. It was an exciting prospect to not only progress in her career and be a part of something that would leave a lasting imprint on the city, but most of all, to be in close proximity to the woman she was so crazy about. As Candice would

Epilogue – 6 weeks later – Ally

pick her up from the airport, she'd gone to a lot more trouble with her appearance than last time, and she'd even managed to squeeze in an appointment with the hairdresser yesterday. Her knee-length black leather pencil skirt, high heels, and crisp, white shirt were highly impractical for a long-haul flight, but now that she was in business class, she'd be able to kick off her shoes and stretch her legs.

She smiled at the ground stewardess who handed over her boarding pass. "I guess it's my lucky day."

"Enjoy your flight, Ms. Brenner. I suggest you head straight for the gate as boarding starts in five minutes."

Ally rushed through security and glanced out of the floor to ceiling widows as she walked to the gate. Sleek planes in Air Canada's signature red-and-white livery stood parked in front of a patchwork runways. Behind those, the concrete airfield was dwarfed by the mountains that dramatically rose up in the distance. The profile of the North Shore Mountains dominated the view, their snow-capped peaks scraping the clouds. It would be a while before she'd be back here; she'd promised her parents she'd visit twice a year, but apart from that, she had no reason to return anytime soon. It felt bittersweet, but she was ready, or as ready as she could be.

She hadn't realized she was in the exact same seat as last time until she'd boarded, and her stomach fluttered, remembering that life-changing flight with Candice. It felt symbolic, somehow, like she'd been on a journey of self-discovery, and she'd come full circle.

"Hey, beautiful."

The familiar voice evoked an intense physical reaction, and Ally gasped when she saw Candice. "What? What are you doing here?" She stared at her. "How long have you been in Vancouver? Why didn't you tell me you were here?"

Epilogue – 6 weeks later – Ally

"I only flew in last night." Candice shot her a sweet smile. "I thought it would be fun to join you."

Ally frowned, still baffled at the absurdity of the situation. Candice was dressed down today, and she looked stunning in jeans and a gray cashmere jumper. She'd missed her so much that the weeks without her had felt like months. "You flew all the way here just so you could fly back with me?"

"I wanted a do-over." Candice sat next to Ally, turned to her, and extended her hand. "Hi," she said. "I'm Candice Blackwater and I upgraded you so you would sit next to me."

Ally giggled as she shook her hand. "It's nice to meet you. I'm Ally Brenner." She laughed even harder when Candice lifted her hand and kissed it. "Are you flirting with me, Ms. Blackwater?"

"Yes. Is that okay?"

Ally couldn't stop smiling. "Yes. But I'm warning you. I will flirt back."

"That's a deal." Candice leaned in, cupped her face, and kissed her tenderly. "We have seven and a half hours. That should be more than enough time to have some fun," she murmured against Ally's mouth.

Ally closed her eyes and ran a hand through Candice's hair while she lost herself in the kiss. It felt heavenly to finally be close to her again, to smell her and feel her and hear her voice in her ear. "I've missed you," she whispered, only inching back when a flight attendant appeared with Champagne.

Clearly a little startled from the display of affection, the woman stared at them for a beat, then painted on a smile. "Welcome, ladies. Would you like a glass of Champagne?"

"Yes, please," Candice said, helping herself. "And I'm

Epilogue – 6 weeks later – Ally

sure my gorgeous girlfriend will have one too." She took another glass off the tray and winked as she handed it to Ally. "We have a lot to celebrate, after all."

"Girlfriend?" Ally blushed, heated from both the kiss and Candice's statement.

"Yeah. My girlfriend. Can I call you that?" Candice grinned. "I know we're two grown women, not a couple of kids trading notebook doodles behind the teacher's back, but I can't shake the need for you to check the 'yes' or 'no' box." She shrugged humorously. "The adult overthinker in me demands it."

Ally fell back in her seat and pressed a hand against her chest over her heart, staring at Candice in adoration. "That's the cutest thing you've said to me." She made a tick in the air with her finger. "Yes!" Although the word "girlfriend" made her blush, she loved the sound of it. She was in love with Candice, a gorgeous and captivating woman who was now officially her partner. A woman who made her feel all the feels each time she looked into her eyes. She'd found clarity in those blue eyes, and somehow, in the short time they'd known each other, they'd restored her trust in love and in her own judgement. With a little nudge, destiny had woven their paths together with delicate precision. Candice was her endgame.

AFTERWORD

I hope you've loved reading Chance Encounters as much as I've loved writing it. If you've enjoyed this book, would you consider rating it and reviewing it? Reviews are very important to authors and I'd be really grateful!

ABOUT THE AUTHOR

Lise Gold is an author of lesbian romance. Her romantic attitude, enthusiasm for travel and love for feel good stories form the heartland of her writing. Born in London to a Norwegian mother and English father, and growing up between the UK, Norway, Zambia and the Netherlands, she feels at home pretty much everywhere and has an unending curiosity for new destinations. She goes by 'write what you know' and is often found in exotic locations doing research or getting inspired for her next novel.

Working as a designer for fifteen years and singing semi-professionally, Lise has always been a creative at heart. Her novels are the result of a quest for a new passion after resigning from her design job in 2018.

When not writing from her kitchen table, Lise can be found cooking, at the gym or singing her heart out somewhere, preferably country or blues. She lives in London with her dogs El Comandante and Bubba.

Sign up to her newsletter: www.lisegold.com

ALSO BY LISE GOLD

Lily's Fire

Beyond the Skyline

The Cruise

French Summer

Fireflies

Northern Lights

Southern Roots

Eastern Nights

Western Shores

Northern Vows

Living

The Scent of Rome

Blue

The Next Life

In The Mirror

Christmas In Heaven

Welcome to Paradise

After Sunset

Paradise Pride

Cupid Is A Cat

Members Only

Along The Mystic River

In Dreams

Under the pen name Madeleine Taylor

The Good Girl

Online

Masquerade

Santa's Favorite

Spanish translations by Rocío T. Fernández

Verano Francés

Vivir

Nada Más Que Azul

Luciérnagas

Hindi translations

Zindagi

Made in United States
North Haven, CT
14 April 2024